FURTHER
BEYOND

A novel by

Valerie Norris

Published by
Llyfrau Cambria Books, Wales, United Kingdom.
Cambria Books is a division of
Cambria Publishing Ltd.
Discover our other books at: www.cambriabooks.co.uk

For my husband, the poet Christopher Norris. Thank you for your love and support, and for writing the interspersed poems.

About the author

In her professional career, Valerie was a Materials Engineer. She was awarded a Royal Society Research Fellowship that took her to Swansea University where she went on to be awarded a Chair, and later became Head of the Materials Research Centre. She took early retirement in 2013. The high point of her career was to be honoured with the title 'Welsh Woman of the Year' in 1998, which led to many activities in public life. In 2004, she was invited to Buckingham Palace as one of the 'Top 180 female achievers in the country'. As well as her novels, she has written and published some 370 research papers and five textbooks in a previous name, Valerie Randle, and has given lectures all over the world. She has achieved an entry in *Who's Who*.

Valerie was born and educated in Kidderminster, England. Wales has been her home since she moved there at the age of eighteen with her first husband. She has been widowed twice and met and married the philosopher-poet Christopher Norris not long after her retirement. She has two children, six grandchildren and three step-grandchildren. Valerie likes to spend her time singing in various acapella groups, long-distance walking, practising yoga and meditation, travelling, learning Spanish and writing. For the last twenty years she has volunteered with Cruse Bereavement Support.

Previous novels by Valerie Norris, also published by Cambria Books:

In the Long Run
The April Letters
Beyond Closure

CONTENTS

Chapter 1	1
Chapter 2	9
Chapter 3	19
Chapter 4	28
Chapter 5	36
Chapter 6	44
Chapter 7	53
Chapter 8	65
Chapter 9	74
Chapter 10	87
Chapter 11	97
Chapter 12	109
Chapter 13	118
Chapter 14	128
Chapter 15	138
Chapter 16	145
Chapter 17	155
Chapter 18	165
Chapter 19	173

Chapter 1

The last time. When was the last time I had known beforehand that something was for 'the last time'? Leaving school was one I could think of, and that was all of forty years ago, give or take. Then by extension there was leaving university. Leaving the various homes I'd lived in didn't really count, because of course I was always going on to another home. It wasn't the end of an era, like this.

I applied my muted lipstick, with half an eye in the mirror at the closed door of one of the toilet stalls behind me. I wanted to escape before whoever she was emerged and I was ambushed in conversation. I didn't want to be forced to paste on my smile prematurely. It only had so much shelf life.

Deep breath and final visual check; a neat blouse under a tailored navy-blue suit and a thin gold chain at my neck. I couldn't help doing a double-take at the half inch of grey at the roots of my hair. Perhaps it was a bit premature, this evidence of slipping standards in the immaculately turned-out professional persona that I had cultivated over the years. On the way to the conference room I stopped by at my desk, swept bare now of its folders, pens, papers, and other office requisites. Only the computer remained. There wasn't much to take home after all these years: a few knick-knacks, tissues and other personal stuff, a grainy picture of Lisa when she was small. She was sitting on a beach, building sandcastles, her blonde hair even more bleached by the sun. Which seaside resort was that? I've no idea now. I peeped through the door into the adjoining room and saw that Janine and the others had already gone. The lure of a Friday afternoon party must have been strong. I knew my role was to make my entrance slightly later, when everyone would have had a chance to get at least one drink under their belts. Time to square my shoulders, lift my chin, and face it. In a couple of hours it would be over. All of it would be over.

The hum of voices – you wouldn't yet call it carousing – was trickling from the conference room. For a second I paused on the threshold, carrying my smile, so that they could notice me. Then their faces lit up, bless them, and they cheered and clapped me in. Dennis came to meet me and brushed a kiss on my cheek, treating me to a whiff of some expensive executive man cologne. He led me to the table which had been set up where Janine and her crew were presiding over champagne, other wines and juices. Champagne! The last time a senior staff member had retired there had been only a choice of red or white.

It was only when I thought about it, sitting woozily on the train afterwards, bag of accumulated office detritus dumped between my feet, that the significance of the champagne choice really had a chance to sink it. It was a sign that I had been appreciated. My memory slid over the party, which had been a success, as these things went. And I'd been to enough of them to know. I had circulated, adroitly fielding the eager and expected 'what are you going to do with yourself now' and 'are you planning a special holiday' inquisitions. I didn't give them any clues. It was like an announcement in a local paper which reports that a bride and groom were going on honeymoon to an 'undisclosed destination'. Do people still do that? Go to an undisclosed destination, that is. Or announce their wedding in a local paper, for that matter.

I had kept up the front while Dennis did his big boss speech and praised my services to the company, spanning more than thirty years. Then the toast. 'To Rhian! The place won't be the same without you, but we wish you many years of happiness in your retirement.' I had been fittingly overwhelmed when he had presented me with a gigantic card, scrawled liberally with signatures and kisses, and a framed picture of woodland by a local artist. Actually, it was lovely. I would certainly give it prominent wall space in my house. Then there was my speech, not too practised, but suitable. I think I hit it right. I didn't imply 'I can't wait to get out of here' or 'don't you wish you were leaving too'. After all, they seemed genuinely pleased for me, not just enjoying an end-of-week party. It wasn't their fault that I had spent the last couple of years feeling like I was wearing a suit of clothes that I had outgrown and was too small for me. But that champagne... that's what had moved me the most. Dennis had dug in the coffers and sent me off with *champagne*. A tribute indeed.

So I had eventually made my final walk down the corridor, picture clutched under my arm. At the last minute it occurred to me to check in the cleaners' closet to make sure I had taken my spare raincoat that I kept there. I must have entered quietly, because I didn't distract the couple at the back behind the buckets and cleaning paraphernalia at all. They were kissing and groping each other enthusiastically. After my first shock I smiled, not entirely surprised. I recognized them both, and two and two quickly slid together in my brain. But it was definitely none of my business now. I backed out quietly, then in a final moment of mischief, slammed the door noisily.

And now the train was pulling up at my stop. It was less crowded on the platform than usual because it was ahead of the normal commuter time. I was slightly, pleasantly drunk as I walked to my house, breathing in the midsummer day and growing lighter with each step. When I put my key in the lock the first sight to greet me inside the door was my suitcase and scruffy backpack, poised to pick up in the morning when I left for my undisclosed destination.

***

I could have told them where I was going, but the truth was, this was the start of my early retirement and it was important to me that work kept its tentacles out of my new life. At the party they had said when I circulated round to one of the groups, all loosened ties and glasses emptying, that they were laying bets on where I was going for my post-retirement holiday. They had probed sneakily, asking about how much jet lag I thought I would get, what clothes I was taking, how long it took to get my visa, etc. I remained loftily enigmatic and managed to field each question with humour. I was getting to enjoy the game. Then someone came up with Machu Pichu, since they knew I had spent several holidays in the last few years trekking on long distance paths in this country and abroad. That was a good time to leave them and drift to another group.

For practical reasons I had told my neighbour (plant watering), Lisa (security) and Cameron (dinner reservations) that I was away for two weeks, and it would have been churlish not to say where I was going. But I hadn't mentioned it to friends, because I had this fear that somebody might say, 'Ooh, I've always wanted to do that, but I haven't had anyone to go with. Can I join you?' It has always puzzled me that a lot of women won't do things on their own. To me, it was bliss. No small talk, no interruptions, just simple immersion in what you were doing. Don't get me wrong, I still needed a certain amount of interaction with friends and family, but increasingly what I craved was interaction with me.

Somewhat to my surprise, Cameron had volunteered to drive me to the station. It seemed that a window had opened up in his Saturday morning calendar, and he could fit me in between his scheduled workout routine at the gym and something in Reading later on in the morning. We were going to eat breakfast together at Reading Station. From there, I would hop on the train heading west to Wales. Yes, Wales. My colleagues – ex-colleagues now – had been way off the mark with their speculations of exotic places. But not so off the mark when they suspected an active holiday.

'You can take this as a pretty poor substitute for the celebration dinner I didn't buy you last night,' said Cameron. We sat at a table in the station concourse, poking paper straws through the lids of our chilled orange juice. I understood that straws had to be paper nowadays, but they always went so squidgy. The station was surprisingly busy, I thought, for a Saturday morning, given the absence of the weekday swarm of commuters, and the long school holidays still weeks away. Nevertheless, there were travellers of several nationalities laden with suitcases, holdalls and backpacks, peering anxiously at the Departures board. Where were they all going?

I brought my attention back to our table and Cameron's remark. 'Last night wouldn't have been the best time for me,' I said. 'I'd already had a fair bit of champagne at the party, and I needed to finish my packing and get an early night. But I appreciate the thought.'

Cameron grunted and bit into his bacon and egg bap. He was never very keen on having his plans thwarted, so it was a good idea to mollify him. 'We'll do something after you've come back,' he said. 'We could even have a long weekend away. How about Italy? Shall I get Mandy to look into it?'

I told him that would be nice. I meant it; three or four nights together in some classy location generally suited us. There would inevitably be a mix of time spent together seeing sights, dining out, and having very acceptable sex, and time spent separately with Cameron glued to his messages or working out, and me reading or just relaxing in the ambience. It worked.

He eyed my modest suitcase and day backpack. 'You're travelling light for a whole fortnight away. Most women would need that much space for their shoes alone.'

'I never need much when I'm walking. Rainwear of course,' – I indicated my lightweight jacket – 'And I wear the same old comfy kit for several days. Then I need a couple of light dresses for the evenings, plus only one pair of shoes.' I emphasised the shoes bit. 'I'm moving to a new place every night, remember.'

He shook his head. 'Well, I'm glad you don't go all spartan like this when you go away with me.'

'I wouldn't dare,' I said, teasing him. 'Anyway, I probably could have taken more, but I'm not used to having my luggage magically transferred for me every night. This trip, with the luggage pick-up, is my post-retirement treat. Usually, I have to carry it all myself so I need to stick to essentials.' Plus there was something cleansing, freeing, about paring your belongings down to a minimum for a couple of weeks. But I didn't challenge Cameron's sophistication by attempting to explain this. He was

5

separate from that part of me.

'That's an interesting business opportunity, organizing accommodation and luggage transfer along a route. I would expect it to be mainly visitors from other countries who take advantage of it. Do you pay a hefty surcharge for the privilege?' I could see the sharp gleam of possibilities in his face. But it was a handsome face, at that. Interesting angles topped with grey, abundant hair which was always expertly trimmed. And a toned, slim body, as you would expect from all that time at the gym. Not very tall, but there I had learned to be tactful. More than one person had said when we first started dating a year or so ago that we made a good-looking couple, me and my toy boy. I say that, when in fact he's fifty-eight, so only a couple of years younger than me.

'I can't really remember what I paid – it's months ago that I booked. But it wasn't outrageous.'

He nodded absently. Already his mind had passed on to something else.

On an impulse I said, 'You don't get this, do you? Me going on long distance treks on my own.' It was said lightly, musingly. The last thing I wanted was a disagreement just minutes before I set off.

He drained the last of his coffee and mopped his mouth with his paper napkin. You didn't see many men do that. 'Honest answer? No, I don't get it. But it's not me who's doing it.' He closed the conversation by looking at his watch. It was time to go.

We were almost at the turnstile, me with my ticket ready in my hand, when he unexpectedly added, 'What I do understand is a person's urge to return to their roots now and again. I suppose I quite envy you your cultural identity. Me, I'm just another London lad, but you, Rhian, you're a Celt. The real deal.'

***

Sometimes we would go to stay with Auntie in Carmarthen. We would climb on the train at Cardiff, which had come all the way from London where the Queen lived, and ride to Swansea where we had to get off. We had to get off because it was the last station, and because the track that the train went on really did stop. It just ended. We went into the station on the train, but trains didn't come out on the other side like normal stations. I was worried that the train might not stop, and we would go crashing into those posts with red lights on at the end. I never said anything about this. Mam was always busy picking up all our things and the boys would just have laughed at me like they always did.

But when we were all off the train at Swansea, there would be another train sitting somewhere else, waiting for us. This was a little train, much smaller than the one that had come all the way from London. And do you know what? This train would go out of the station the same way ours had just come in. Because there was nowhere else for it to go. So we could go beyond Swansea after all. We went beyond. Carmarthen was beyond. Carmarthen wasn't like Cardiff, where streets were full of cars and there were lots of people. Instead, it was quiet where Auntie lived and the people talked funny. I liked Auntie.

Then sometimes, when the weather was hot and the leaves on the trees waved at us, we got back on the train at Carmarthen, but we didn't come home. Instead we went further beyond. Now when you looked out of the windows you didn't see houses, but fields and cows and sheep and rivers. When I sat on Mam's lap I could see it all properly, and she would whisper stories about it in my ear. But she kept having to stop because the boys were fighting. They were always fighting. Dad was there when we went further beyond, but he didn't stop the boys fighting. He just read his newspaper and pretended it wasn't happening.

After we had eaten our sandwiches the train stopped and we all had to get off because the land had finished and there was only sea, and a big white boat. The big white boat sailed off, but we stayed.

***

Craning my head out of the window while the train pulled unhurriedly into Swansea, I could watch the station gradually magnify in front of me. And there it was! The train which was to

7

chug its way west was waiting on the next platform, all three carriages of it, looking puny compared to the long monstrosity which was delivering me from Reading.

I swung my suitcase onto the luggage rack in the second train. Getting a window seat facing forwards was easy; the train was only about one-third full. Whereas there must have been changes in the rolling stock, the signage in the station and the turnstiles at the exit, the main thing that lingered with me was climbing down off the big train and running the few yards across the platform to the little one, with Mam telling me to be careful. Had I journeyed three hours from Reading or half a century?

The guard's whistle shrieked, the train gave a lurch, and we were moving. The welcome Welsh accent told me over the loudspeaker which stations we were calling at. Why had it taken me so long to remake this magical journey? Over the years we had taken a couple of holidays in Pembrokeshire, Wales' western tip, when Lisa was little. But we didn't even consider taking the train to get there. It was pile all our gear into the car and hurtle down the motorway, with John driving, until the motorway ran out and we hit scenic A-roads. But how Lisa would have loved being on this train. I would have told her tales of when I was a little girl like her, doing this very same journey. I would have relived it all through her, whereas now I was reliving it on my own. I had an impulse to phone her and ask if she had any memory of our family holidays in Pembrokeshire. But I didn't. You never knew what Lisa's response might be.

Meanwhile, it was going to take a couple of hours until I was disgorged at Tenby, near the southern end of the trail. From there I would hug the rugged Coast Path where it clung to bays, estuaries and rocky promontories, round the toes of Pembrokeshire that protruded out to the west, until I had come round three-quarters of a circle to the trail's northern end, near Cardigan. All 186 miles of it.

Chapter 2

When I rang the doorbell at Lisa's house I could discern noises of yelling, even through the front door. Joe. You had to make allowances for the little chap, though. I hovered, not sure whether to ring again, because Lisa would have her hands full placating him. Unless she hadn't heard the ring above all the din? Funny how it was our custom to use the front door at each other's houses, rather than to go round to the back door and just announce 'hello, it's me' as you barged in. It summed up our relationship.

The hollering was dying down, so I knocked, tentatively. It was Nathan who opened the door and stood back to let me come in. I swear that boy had grown a couple of inches since I last saw him, and that was less than a month ago. Although I suppose we all would prefer our descendants to follow our own side of the family, the older Nathan got, the more he seemed to have the look of his dad about him. His dad is a good-looking bloke, so that worked in his favour. 'Alright? Mum's upstairs with Joe. She won't be long.'

The days when his face would light up when he saw me and give me a huge hug were long gone. Nowadays he bore all the awkwardness that came with adolescence, and he avoided calling me Gran. Not that I ever liked that title, but it's what I am. One of my roles, anyway. Of course, I had chosen to erase one of my roles recently, so there was a vacancy for something new. I was mulling this over, on and off.

I sat down in the living room, which was splattered with Lego, comics and plates smeared with the remains of toast and jam. The TV was on showing some cartoon that I didn't recognise. Nathan hung around, looking lanky and self-conscious. He searched under

9

cushions for the remote then turned the sound down but left the figures cavorting on the screen. I asked him conventional Gran questions about school and what have you, to which he replied politely enough. He was a nice lad.

We were both glad to hear footsteps on the stairs, and to see Lisa shepherding a solemn-looking Joe through the door. I recognised this default look of Joe's, the one that his autism had bestowed on him. I got up so that Lisa and I could exchange kisses. I didn't even try to go there with Joe. I bent down to his level and said hello, but he ignored me and started playing with his Lego. Lisa didn't insist that he greeted me, so I gathered it must have been a bad meltdown.

Lisa moved a pile of papers off an armchair and flopped down in it. 'Bad day?' I said.

'Oh, not so much.' She rubbed her eyes. 'Work's a bit of a pain, but then, what's new? Put the kettle on, will you, Nath?'

I looked at my daughter. Years of being a single parent to two boys, one with special needs, while holding down a job, had taken their toll. That vivacious, cheeky sparkle that used to be her hallmark had gradually been eroded and replaced by the more sober demeanour of a woman in her mid-thirties, slightly plump and frayed around the edges. Perhaps some of that was no more than what time and life would have bestowed on her anyway. I should know.

'So how was your trip?'

How was my trip. A few words to frame a simple question with a momentous answer. I had been back home only one day, and I felt dislocated, unsettled, unwilling to re-engage with my life. I know you always feel like that after a good holiday; it takes a few days to totally sink into your normal routine again. But this was different. A few days wasn't going to do it because I had no regular routine to fit back into now. It was what I had chosen.

'My trip. It was… it was everything I hoped it would be and more.' My pause wasn't for dramatic effect, it was because I didn't know how to articulate what I felt.

Lisa raised her eyebrows. 'Wow, high praise. It all worked out then – getting your case transferred, finding your place to stay every evening, finding places to eat, all that stuff?'

'Like a dream. The accommodation was simple guest houses, and many of them provided an evening meal and sent you off with a packed lunch the next morning. Not any menu choice, but good substantial food. Which was just what you wanted when you were hungry after a day's walking.'

'What about the weather? Did it rain at all?'

'Not much. I was lucky.'

Lisa twiddled a lock of her hair that had slipped loose from the scrunchy that she often wore. 'You said it was everything you hoped it would be and more. What does that mean, exactly?' To be fair, she was making an effort to be interested, given that long-distance walking wasn't her thing at all.

I sipped at the mug of coffee that Nathan had brought in and thought how to reply. 'You see, I wanted something to… to get the last residues of my working life out of my bones. I wanted fresh air, open spaces, being by the sea, the horizon, freedom, solitude. Time to think, time to absorb, time to plan my next move.' I stopped before I got even more carried away. I recognised that look. It was the 'Mum's being a bit weird but you have to bear with her' look. Do most mothers of adult kids encounter that look?

'Me, I'd rather have a week away lying on a beach and drinking plenty of cocktails with the girls.'

A memory of what had befallen when she did just that a few years ago crossed my mind but I pushed it out again. Instead, I turned my attention to Joe, who was playing quietly on the rug with his Lego.

'What are you making, Joe?' I said. 'Do you want to show me?' No response.

Lisa joined in the encouragement. 'Come on, Joe. Granny would like to see.'

I dropped down on the floor beside him and picked up a few of the brightly coloured bricks, feeling their corners and edges. 'It's a lorry,' he said eventually, without lifting his eyes from where his little fingers were deftly adding new pieces.

11

'So it is. I can see its wheels and everything. It's ever so good.' I knew better than to push him too much, so I sat back down on the sofa.

'Do you remember going to Pembrokeshire when you were little?' I said to Lisa. 'We went there for a couple of holidays.'

She shook her head. 'I have memories of you and Dad taking me to lots of different places with beaches, but I couldn't tell you whereabouts they were. We went away every summer, didn't we?'

'We certainly did.' I felt obscurely disappointed that she didn't remember. It would have been a point of contact between us, and they were sometimes a bit of a challenge to manufacture.

'Solitude, you said. So you didn't see many people there?'

'It was pretty quiet. I wasn't a hermit, though. I chatted with people in the evening if I went to the pub, and I had quite a long talk with someone on a beach one day.' I thought of the tatty scrap of paper, folded up in my purse, which had a phone number scribbled on it.

Nathan came in, his skateboard under his arm. 'Is it alright if I go down the rec? Gav just messaged.'

Lisa frowned. 'Bit rude when Gran's here, isn't it?'

Nathan gave a look that was halfway between crestfallen and mutinous. 'It's OK,' I said quickly. 'You go out and enjoy yourself.' Why would a fifteen-year-old lad want to be stuck in talking to his grandmother, especially if she was considered to be a bit eccentric.

'Well, alright,' said Lisa. 'But remember, I want you to be back in plenty of time for tea today.' She said this with emphasis, fixing him with a stare.

'Oh yeah. I will.'

We heard the backdoor slam as he went out.

'Well, that's enough about me and my trek. How is everything with you?'

'Oh, pretty good.' She examined her fingernails.

'Would you like me to do any babysitting? Anything lined up?' She shook her head. 'Not at the moment. I'm starting to get Nathan to watch Joe a bit. I'm bribing him with pocket money. Oh, and guess what, I found a girl who's experienced with autistic kids and looking for a bit of money by babysitting. She came once while you were away and it worked really well. Joe liked her.'

I nearly said that she didn't need to go throwing her money away on babysitters when I'd done that sometimes, as far as my job would let me, but then I held back. Who knew where my new life might lead me?

For the next half an hour she filled me in with more about the boys and what they were up to. As I drove back home, I was thoughtful. There was something I couldn't put my finger on. Lisa had seemed evasive, slightly tense, and unwilling to meet my eyes. Was it something in her, or was I projecting the unrest that was seething in me?

**

'Here's to your retirement, Rhian. May it be long and happy.' We clinked glasses and drank deeply. No wussy sipping for us; although we were far from being connoisseurs, both Cameron and I appreciated wine. We were ensconced in a corner of a rather upmarket, minimalist-decor restaurant, which was Cameron's treat to me to mark my retirement. He had booked a taxi to bring me here, and there would be another to whisk us back to his place afterwards. It was all rather agreeable.

It was the first time we'd met since I'd come back, and Cameron asked if it had been a success overall. We'd been in touch a few times while I was away, but that had mostly been short messages with me giving a bulletin on my progress. With Cameron it tended to be 'out of sight, out of mind', and we were both capable of filling our time without pining for the other. It was a grown-up relationship.

So I did my best, in between appreciating mouthfuls of excellent risotto, to give him a short overview of the whole trip. I talked about the breathtaking magnificence of the coast, and how it became even more dramatic and wild as you slogged your way further beyond the miniature city of St Davids towards Strumble

Head, then Fishguard, and finally Cardigan. He didn't seem bored at all. He asked questions, which were all technical, such as how many miles I did per day, what was my average pace, how much water did I take on board. This interest in fitness and how to quantify it chimed with what I knew about Cameron. In fact I had always known this, even going back to before I had met him, because his dating site profile proclaimed him to have '*an ardent interest in sport and keeping fit. I confess I'm quite obsessive about logging my training and analysing it'.* Something like that, anyway, if my memory serves. At the time it had struck a chord with me that this was a man who was likely to have a good physique and also to be well organised. I wasn't wrong.

It dawned on me that he was curious about the whole discipline of long-distance walking. 'Wouldn't you like to do some long-distance walking yourself? Apart from being damn good exercise, it's food for your soul, you know.' I was half teasing. 'Life boils down to such simplicity. For those few days everything you do is centred on just one thing – getting from A to B under your own steam. When you're not walking you're only doing activities that support the walking, like resting, sleeping, sorting your kit, planning the next day or refuelling.'

'Me? Come off it. When would I have the time to go gallivanting off like that? I'll stick with running and working out at the gym, thank you. And anyway, you know I haven't got a soul.'

I let that one go. It was a discussion we'd had before. Instead I pulled out my phone and showed him some pictures, which were mainly sea, cliffs, bays and sky. And the horizon. Horizons fascinated me: that amalgam of sea and sky was a magical place. But the small two-dimensional view onscreen couldn't do any of it justice. 'It really is an amazing part of the world,' I said, feeling like I was overselling now. 'If you're going to be tackling a long walk, you may as well have some splendour to immerse yourself in.'

'I still think it's to do with your Welsh heritage. I told you, I'm dead jealous.'

I thought about this. 'I don't honestly know. I do feel some connection with Pembrokeshire, and I remember going there as a child on holidays, but it was Cardiff where I lived until I went to university, and I don't feel any special pull for that place. I've got a couple of cousins there and that's it. I never go there now.'

We were sitting back finishing our wine, the second bottle actually, and digesting our excellent main course before we contemplated the dessert menus that had been laid in front of us. 'Do you plan to do any more long-distance walks now that you have all this free time?' he said.

'I haven't given that any thought, but what I am going to do is to go back to Pembrokeshire soon, particularly the north, and devote some time to exploring. I didn't see enough of it. Most of my day was spent walking on the coast, so I didn't get much idea of the interior, or of the villages. I want to linger.' As I rolled the word round my mouth, I could feel a yearning welling up in me. To linger. I had time now. Tomorrow I would get that tatty piece of paper out of my purse.

'I don't see you as a lingerer. Not for long, anyway.'

'What do you see me as?'

Cameron took a mouthful of wine and I sat calm and inscrutable under his shrewd appraisal. We were both good at this sort of game. 'I think within six months you'll be out of your skull with boredom and you'll either be doing consultancy or have set up your own business.'

I laughed. 'You're way off the mark.' We eyed each other, enjoying the challenge.

He cracked first. 'Give me a clue.'

I considered. 'Something I've never done, had a hankering to do for a few years but never really had the time and space. Mental space, that is.'

'Mental space?' He frowned while he thought. 'Are you going to do some course or other? A higher degree? Write a book?' He sounded doubtful, but he wasn't a million miles away.

I felt my heartbeat start to increase, nervous now that I was about to reveal my aspiration to someone for the first time.

'I'm going to write poetry.'

The landscape of chrome and glass in Cameron's open-plan kitchen was almost dazzling on a bright morning like this. You felt like you needed sunglasses. His cleaning lady (housekeeper, he had corrected me) must spend half her time polishing it to make it gleam like that. I was perched on a white leather stool at the kitchen counter, my hand curled around my second cappuccino of the day. Now, I'm not a total stranger to kitchen appliances, but Cameron had to give me a tutorial on how to work the coffee machine. It was worth it though; that was one killer coffee.

This was the first time I had been in Cameron's flat on my own, so I could be thoroughly nosy and investigate to my heart's content. I could take in the generous proportions of the integrated kitchen, dining and living area. I could slide open silent drawers and see serried ranks of cutlery, forks and spoons curled into each other. I could stand at the window – which took up most of the one side of the flat – and gaze at tiny cars crawling far below, with distant glimpses of the silvery river. As well as all that, I could really have a good peruse of the photographs featuring Cameron's two sons. There were degree ceremonies, a wedding (with the brother as best man) and several of intrepid physical activities in exotic-looking locations. You could definitely see the likeness to their dad.

This morning while I was still buried under the fluffy duvet Cameron had kissed me on the cheek, smelling of toothpaste, before heading to the gym and his office. He reiterated that I could help myself to anything I wanted and not bother with any clearing up; his cleaner – sorry, housekeeper – would see to it all. So I had luxuriated in bed a while longer, pondering the still incredible fact that the days were gone when I would be flinging myself into my clothes and rushing out to catch the train.

I eventually took myself to the bathroom, which seemed like an extension of the kitchen in terms of innovation and white stylishness. The shower had a range of controls that you could operate to get various jets, deluges or mists on different parts of your body. I tried them all. Honestly, this place would give a five-star hotel a run for its money. And don't get me started on the fridge with all its computer-controlled options.

We had tended to spend more of our together time here than at my house. That was always supposed to be because here was more convenient for the sort of places we liked to go out to, but now I wonder. Did Cameron find my house, a bog-standard three-bedroomed semi in a suburb, a bit primitive after all this state-of-the-art luxury? Or maybe he found it warmer and more homely after this rather sterile environment? Anyway he seemed to like having a Sunday lunch cooked for him. I tried to think objectively about my house, which takes some effort when you've lived there for going on a quarter of a century. It had been the marital home, but I had chosen to buy John out and stay there after he had cleared off and we divorced. God knows why, looking back. Oh, I redecorated it all through, got new furniture, made it my own. But that was years ago, and I'd done virtually nothing since. I cast my mind's eye over the comfortable shabbiness that cocooned me – the tottering piles of books, the cheerfully cluttered kitchen, the stuffed cupboards. It could all definitely do with a declutter and a makeover, which I'd managed to put to the back of my mind. However now, at the start of my retirement, I supposed was the time to tackle it. It wasn't my favourite sort of thing.

To distract myself from these tiresome considerations, I persuaded my thoughts to return to when I had dropped the bombshell last evening about my ambitions in the world of poetry. I had tried to describe, stumblingly, that for a few years now I had turned to reading poetry as an alternative to novels. And I found that it touched my soul like no other words could. From there it was just a step to wanting, and trying, to conjure up some poetry myself. But a working life consumed by the treadmill of spreadsheets, audits, tax returns and the like didn't leave enough time or mental spaciousness to engage properly with this endeavour. I say that my explanation to Cameron came haltingly both because I was met with total bafflement from him, and also because of my own inadequacy to articulate in words what I truly meant. Which is ironic, when you come to think about it, since it was words that I yearned to spend time exploring.

Eventually Cameron digested what I had said and cottoned on to the fact that an end-product of my ventures could be a book. Something that was marketable. This he understood, so he went waffling on about the little he knew concerning publishers and royalties, which so much missed the point for me. I didn't want pressure, targets, goals. What I craved was the freedom and conditions to have a go, to fulfil this burgeoning need which bubbled inside me. So I had smiled sweetly, said it was just an idea I'd had, not fixed, and changed the subject. We both breathed a sigh of relief.

But the truth was, it had become an important part of my inner life. Nowadays it was always present within me like an underground stream. A couple of years ago I had found a local poetry group, held in the upstairs room of a pub. I went a few times, on my own, as if it was some rehab group, almost a dirty secret. I didn't even ask any friend to go with me, mainly because I couldn't think of anyone it would appeal to. I had written a few short poems by this point, but I wasn't brave enough to expose them at the poetry evenings. Instead, I listened to other people's offerings. And dreamed.

Chapter 3

One of the greetings cards I had when I retired was from an old university friend. In it she had written *banish the word 'should' from your vocabulary*. Sound advice. Which is why I was sitting in my garden in the sunshine reading a book of poetry by Rumi rather than cleaning my house which is what I should – I mean *could* – have been doing. My garden is small but sufficient: a lawn, a few shrubs and a tiny patio. It's easy for me to maintain on my own. I immersed myself in the ancient words of Rumi's verses, which called to me from over the centuries. After a while I put the book down. There was only so much I could absorb in one sitting.

The ring of my mobile brought me back to the present. Lisa.

'Hi Mum, how are you? I hope I'm not disturbing you?'

'I'm fine, and not at all. What's up?' Some last minute childcare, most likely. She was using her cheery please-can-you voice.

'Would you be able to meet me for a drink? Say tomorrow, eight o'clock?'

That was unexpected. 'Yes, I think so. Is everything OK?'

'Oh yes, everything's fine. I've got some news.'

I tried my best to get her to put me out of my suspense but she said she didn't want to discuss it over the phone. I did manage to get her to say that it was good news, but surprising. That fitted in with the way her voice seemed to hold both excitement and trepidation. I asked her who was going to be staying with the kids, and she said that was all taken care of. It was most mysterious.

I sat mulling this over, while a blackbird came and joined me at the far end of the lawn. He was quite a frequent visitor, and it always gave me pleasure to watch him pecking speculatively at the grass. Good news, she had said. A new job? She hadn't mentioned anything was in the offing. A windfall? Well, that would be nice. A new romance? She didn't usually tell me much about her love life. There had been a boyfriend quite recently, but it had ended abruptly. I had babysat a few times and she had been dressed up to look her best for a date with this guy. Oh no – she couldn't be pregnant, could she? That would explain why it was too momentous to tell me on the phone.

I put my book down and absorbed this shocking thought. It was certainly possible. At least this time she would know who the father was and she would get support. My mind turned to seven years ago when she had gone away to Magaluf and come back expecting Joe. I had pleaded with her then to have the pregnancy terminated. But she had been adamant that she was keeping the baby, even with a failed marriage behind her and one child already. I remembered how it had struck me that she had been serene, you could say almost joyful, about her pregnancy, even though it brought a lot of complications. To be fair, her ex-husband rallied round and helped her, as did I. I was working in the daytime, but I gave some financial support and took care of Nathan and Joe sometimes on a weekend. But surely now with two boys, one of them a bit of a handful, Lisa wouldn't want another child. Would she?

***

Yes, I definitely needed to return to Pembrokeshire sometime, to join the dots of my speedy foray around its coast. It had teased my nature taste buds and I was hungering for more. This time I fancied setting down temporary roots – can you have 'temporary roots?' – somewhere and exploring from there. The thing was, where to choose? There were small towns, villages, beaches both sandy and stony, dramatic cliffs and rocky inlets. In fact one of the things that makes Pembrokeshire so beguiling is the subtle variation in scenery and ambiance as you traverse from the English-influenced south to the wild Welsh-dominated north. I had been ruminating on this while I was savouring my packed lunch on a small beach called Pwllgwaelod, having departed that morning from Fishguard and set my feet to travel north. The Coast Path laid itself out in splendour in front of me, and my destination that evening was the village of Newport. It was the penultimate day of my adventure, and I didn't want it to end.

Pwllgwaelod turned out to be a lazily pretty cove, a good spot for launching small boats and canoes, with a steep descent from the clifftop on one side and the imposing hump of Dinas Head on the other. It faced west, into the prevailing wind, so the waves that washed up onto its dark greyish sand were quite frisky, given that there was a fair breeze today. You could see all the way back along the route I had just walked, right to the harbour in Fishguard, some miles away. The ferry from Ireland, the big white boat of my childhood, had sauntered its way in and was now awaiting a new batch of passengers. My memory of seeing this big white boat was clear, although I don't suppose we had ever stayed in Fishguard, so I'm not sure how that fits in with my recollections. Sometimes what you think of as your memories don't represent the real truth.

My musings were interrupted by two things happening almost at once: a woman's voice yelling 'Benton! Benton! Here, boy!' and a hairy small dog almost landing on top of me in an attempt to be friendly. Now I don't mind dogs, but this one was a bit in your face – literally. I fended him off, laughing. He wasn't the least bit perturbed and gambolled back to his mistress who was puffing towards me. They say that dogs can get to look like their owners, and since this woman had untidy grey hair and was slightly plump, it was probably true.

'Benton! Naughty boy!' Benton ignored his telling off. 'I must apologise. He doesn't usually do that.'

She seemed really flustered about the encounter so I sought to defuse the situation. 'There's no harm done. At least I'd finished my sandwiches.'

'I've always done my best to get him to behave but he's still too exuberant sometimes.' I was a bit nonplussed when the woman plonked herself down beside me. You wouldn't get that happening in the Southeast. But then, there wasn't any place like Pwllgwaelod in the Southeast. 'Are you walking on the Coast Path?' She definitely had all the friendliness and directness of a typical Welsh person, but her accent wasn't Welsh; more a refined English.

'Yes, I am.' She seemed to be waiting for more information so I added that today I was heading for Newport. She enthused over what a beautiful walk that was going to be and filled me in on some of the delightful sights I had coming up for the afternoon, such as Cwm Yr Eglwys where the waterside church had been mainly washed into the sea during great storms years ago, and a couple of bays that were only accessible on foot.

Well, I could afford to take a few more minutes over my lunch break so I dropped my guard – it's quite normal practice to be reserved around strangers where I live – and relaxed into the conversation. Soon she had extracted from me that I was walking the entire Coast Path for the first time, that I lived in England and that I was just blown away by the awesomeness of the experience.

As she drew breath to ask another question, I grabbed the conversational ball and asked her if she lived around here.

The breeze blew strands of her disorderly hair across her face and she brushed it back. Not that I was in any position to criticise unkempt appearance; the only time I had looked in the mirror during this fortnight was to put my contact lenses in. 'Yes, this is my backyard. I live a few miles inland,' she indicated vaguely with her hand. 'We fancied a quieter life so we upped sticks moved here a few years ago from London. So now all this is home.' She sounded smug, but then, who wouldn't? We both fell silent for a minute and took in the vista before us that presented itself like a picture. A man in a wet suit was just carrying a paddle board down to launch in the sea. It seemed a bit wavy to me for stand-up paddling, but I guess he knew what he was doing.

Benton ran around in circles on the sand in front of us, coming back periodically to gaze adoringly at his mistress, while keeping a suspicious eye on me. My theory was that he had mistaken me for someone else, and now the little fellow was confused because presumably my scent didn't fit. I said to her that I envied her for living here, and part of me meant it. 'I would like to come back later this summer for another trip so that I can take my time and explore in more detail,' I said. 'Probably somewhere in this area rather than in the south.' She agreed that North Pembrokeshire certainly had a charm all of its own.

'I know someone who is just renovating a cottage, quite near the coast, to be rented out soon. It sleeps two, I believe. Would you be interested?' She turned to me, her expression eager, or should I say even more eager. She really did seem like a nice lady. 'I don't know,' I said. 'Possibly.' Nice or not, my habitual caution with a stranger reasserted itself. Although I had to admit that a little cottage, nestling snugly in a green valley somewhere round here, did sound beguiling.

The bottom line was that before I had hefted my backpack onto my shoulders a few minutes later, I had in my purse a phone number, scrawled on a tatty bit of paper, getting even more tatty each time I took it out to look at it.

***

Just parking. Be there soon x

I responded with *OK x*. Not that Lisa had needed to contact me to say she was on her way, because it wasn't quite eight o'clock yet. But we both shared the value of punctuality. I think it was the first time that had occurred to me. Probably if I thought about it I would find that we had other shared values.

It was a respectable old-fashioned pub, with pictures of nature scenes on the walls and an open fireplace. Being midweek, it was quite quiet. There were two tables occupied by couples having a meal, and a foursome who looked like they had already eaten. From the Bar beyond this room you could hear the noise of lads' banter, and even see a darts' board. As I said, an old-fashioned pub, worthy of the name.

'Hello Mum.' Lisa leaned over to kiss me breathlessly on the cheek. She was looking casual in ripped jeans and a loose T-shirt, her face slightly pink from the hurrying. It must be a sign of my age that I don't get ripped jeans. Yet it's a fashion that seems to have hung around for a while and Lisa wore them very becomingly. They were not too tight and yet fitted well enough to accentuate her curves. While she settled herself I went to the bar to get her a glass of house red, which was her usual tipple and what she'd asked for. Well, that eliminated one possibility from my list of topics for her hot news: she obviously wasn't pregnant.

'So who's looking after the boys tonight?' Lisa took her time swallowing her first mouthful and putting her glass back down on the table.

'Simon,' she said.

'That's good he could come.' To be fair, Lisa's ex-husband always had plenty of contact with Nathan, and Joe too. And the arrangement of when and how often he saw Nathan was pretty elastic, which seemed to suit everyone.

'Actually, he was there already.' Lisa dropped her eyes down to the table and rotated the stem of her wineglass.

'Oh?' I was mystified that she should seem uncomfortable. I waited for clarification.

'You see Mum, Simon's moved in.' Lisa lifted her head up and I could see both apprehension and bravado in her expression. 'I guess that must be a bit of a surprise.'

At first I didn't speak. Of all the scenarios I had run in my head, this was not one of them. You wouldn't have your ex-husband of thirteen years move back in with you. It just didn't happen. Lisa and Simon had always been civil to each other, even friendly, for Nathan's sake, but living together again? No. I asked her for some explanation.

'Several weeks ago Simon called round because he was a bit depressed and he'd had some work problems. I was feeling sorry for myself too because the man I was seeing had just dumped me. So we... well, we comforted each other.'

'What do you mean, 'comforted each other?''

She looked me in the eye. 'I mean we slept together and he stayed the night. The boys were away. Joe was with you, as I

24

remember.' I said nothing.

'The next morning Simon was all for starting to see each other again straightaway, but I was confused by what had just gone on and I wanted to take it more slowly. So we did. As it happened, he was going away for a couple of weeks, so that gave me a chance to step back and think. It was so strange, this man who was both so familiar and yet new to me, both at the same time. Anyway, when he came back from his holiday, we went out a few times without telling the boys, and he started coming round a bit more. A couple of times he stayed over and slept on the sofa. The boys just took that in their stride, and they loved having him there. And how we talked! He would phone and message me every day. Sometimes–'

I couldn't keep quiet any longer. 'How can you have forgotten that this man left you when Nathan was a toddler?' I could feel the bewilderment and anger building up inside me.

'We've both grown up and changed so much since then. You must admit Simon's always been good with Nathan, and Joe too. And he's rallied round with extra money, and even treated Joe like his own son. Which is a huge thing to have done.'

I just sat back and looked at her. I couldn't take it in.

She twiddled a lock of her hair, always a sign that she was anxious.

'Mum, I would never have forecast this a few months ago. But honestly, it just grew. We had been getting more and more onto a friendly footing as each year went by, but I never in a million years expected this… I didn't expect to fall in love with the Simon as he is now. Because that's what's happened. It's like a miracle, or a dream.' Her face broke into a big smile, and she reached over and took my hand. 'Please be happy for me.' The quintessential woman in love. Then she played her trump card. 'He moved in with me a week ago and the boys are just ecstatic about it. For Joe to be that excited about anything is unheard of. Simon plans to sell his flat and then we can look round for a new house. A nicer, bigger place, for all four of us. We might get a dog.'

Well, it would all be a good thing for the boys, I supposed. Provided it worked, and it wasn't the product of a temporary sexual infatuation. But if it didn't work out… there would be a lot of pieces to pick up. It was one hell of a gamble. I said this much to her.

'We both know that. So it *has* to work. But, Mum, it feels so right. I'm happier than I've been for years.'

There certainly was a glow about her in her earnestness to convince me. I wanted to share her joy, but I had too many misgivings.

A smell of steak assailed us as a couple of steaming platters arrived at the table next to us. The pub was obviously doing well. The inconsequential thought came into my head that I don't eat good, honest pub food anymore. When I went out with Cameron or with friends it was always to restaurants or wine bars.

I broke the silence. 'I want to wish you well. I *do* wish you well, but I can't say I'm not concerned. Don't you think you're rushing into this a bit?'

Her hopeful expression hardened. 'You've never liked Simon, have you? You've never given him a chance. You were always down on him.'

Hang on a minute… where did all that suddenly come from? Out of the blue she announces the news that he's moved back in and now this bombshell. I couldn't let that pass. 'Aren't you forgetting that I let both you and Nathan move in with me, in quite a small three-bedroomed house? And then after Simon left, I helped you to get on your feet and to get a home of your own?' I knew I was being confrontational but then so was she, and you couldn't blame me for wanting to defend myself.

'It always felt like you didn't want us there. Simon and I not having a place of our own was a big factor in us breaking up, you know.'

I could feel my heartbeat starting to pound. 'Do you think things were easy for me, back then? Your Dad had gone off with that woman not long before. I was struggling to come to terms with being the abandoned wife and at the same time climbing the ladder at work so I could get more financial security. It was a difficult time for me too, Lisa. And it's not true to say that I didn't like

26

Simon. I didn't like it when he left you. I'd had enough of that in my own life.'

I stopped, breathing heavily, stepping back from what I was going to say next. You've only got to open the door to the past an inch and it all starts to spill out. Shut it quickly while you still can.

We both sat back and sipped our wine, afraid of what had been unleashed. 'Look,' I said. 'Let's not dwell on the past. Let's just say back then it was a bad time for all of us. But we've all survived.' I made a big effort and put my concerns aside. 'You and Simon getting back together is amazing news, and I'm sure it will work out splendidly for all four of you.'

Somewhat sheepishly Lisa thanked me. We had smoothed our disagreement over before too much was said. As we often did.

Lisa wisely changed the subject and we talked about other things for a while. Then she said, 'By the way, I saw Dad last week. He hasn't been very well. I told him he should go to the doctor's, but you know what he's like.'

'Oh.' Lisa did tend to tell me snippets of news about John, and I never knew what she expected me to say. I just didn't want to know what was happening with him. He was not part of my life. That's what he had chosen.

Then the thought came to me: Lisa said she had seen him last week. Was that to tell him the news about her and Simon? Surely she hadn't told him before me? It was going to torment me unless I asked her.

There was only one right answer, and she gave it.

27

Chapter 4

I had spent more than a few delicious hours planning my next trip to Pembrokeshire, between catching up with various people, a nice weekend away with Cameron, and tackling a few domestic jobs that loomed as semi-important. Where exactly shall I choose to go, was the first question. I spread my battered Ordnance Survey map of Pembrokeshire out on the table and pored, which was always a very gratifying occupation for me. Of course, using the GPS on your phone was brilliant when you were out and about, or even checking an online map before you left home, but there was a special pleasure to be indulged when you spread out the folds of your paper map and entered in. You saw the big picture, that was the thing, not the bit that could be reduced to a small screen in your hand. My OS map took up half the table. You could see the black railways and red main roads, sometimes with grey buildings clinging to them, which connected the various route centres. The little brown roads and yellow roads and byways wandered with less obvious intent. Then there were the features that man had had no hand in: the intricacies of the twisting coast where the sea had gnawed it into shape, the tracery of streams and rivers, the brown contours which let into your head an image of the rumpled terrain. You know, maybe I could have been a geographer. In another life.

I homed in on Fishguard as the optimal place to stay. It had taken my eye when I had stayed there for one night on my grand coast trek. Fishguard was three small towns in one. There was Lower Town, a picturesque old fishing village at the mouth of the river, the main town of Fishguard, perched on a cliff top with outstanding views out to sea, and Goodwick, whose harbour was the home of the big white ferry. There were also places that I had read about and that looked beguiling on my map. One place that had captured my imagination was a valley called Cwm Gwaun, where the river Gwaun was ushered into the sea at Lower Town. It was a wide, winding ribbon of green on the map, showing wooded terrain. The green was darkened by the overlaid close contours, indicating steep sides to the valley. I longed to see it.

The valleys of my mind
Are deep and green with air of woods unbreathed...

The words shapeshifted in my mind as I tried to get hold of them. Soon I would capture them on the page and let them clarify. But not right now. I was itching to get my next adventure to West Wales booked and on my calendar.

Then there was the question of how long to go away for. A week would fly by, whereas two weeks might be a bit long, especially given the slight tension with Lisa. I didn't want her to read disapproval into my length of stay. But then, when wasn't there a slight background tension between Lisa and me? And I didn't disapprove, as such; she and Simon were both adults and could do as they pleased. It was the boys that concerned me. When I went to visit them yesterday, Nathan was full of the news. Nowadays he is often as taciturn as a fifteen-year-old can be, but then he was bubbling. He lit up with delight as he told me that Dad was living with them. Joe had taken Simon's appearance in his stride, as if it were a natural occurrence. At least that's how it seemed, from the little I could get out of him. Instead, he wanted to tell me more about Ellen, the girl who came to look after him sometimes now. He seemed to have really taken to her. Lisa had invited me round when Simon was out, rather tactfully I thought. One step at a time.

I turned my thoughts back to arranging my trip. Then it came to me: why am I thinking of going away in segments of weeks? So I settled on nine days. A nice boutique hotel in Fishguard with a sea view room and availability for when I was thinking of travelling popped up in my search on booking.com, and I was good to go. I was still drunk on all the freedom I had at my disposal nowadays. I could go for nine days or nineteen if I chose, and I had the comfort of my pension lump sum nestling in the bank.

I felt a bit guilty about going away again without Cameron. I had asked him if he wanted to come and join me for a long weekend. I held my breath while he considered it and weighed up the pros and cons of 'going all that way to see a bit of coast', as he put it. I didn't argue. Eventually he said he'd probably better spend that weekend visiting family, which was overdue. Cameron doesn't belong in West Wales. That's just for me.

***

My boutique hotel had certainly lived up to expectations. The room was not particularly large, but it overlooked the harbour and the sea, so I didn't care. It was a view that you could just drink in. The first thing I had done after I had been led up the stairs by the chatty girl on the desk and shown to my room on the second floor was to drop my baggage and stand at the window. I was open mouthed, taking in every detail of the squat cottages on the quayside, the collection of small boats resting in the harbour, the greenery on the jutting headland and the way the sea blended with the horizon. Half an hour later I had unpacked my belongings, made a cup of tea and was sat in the armchair which was conveniently sited in front of the window. I allowed myself to settle down and then checked my emails, as you do. I hadn't expected the first one that popped up.

Dear Rhian

Hello, it's Simon here. I'm sure that you must be surprised by the news that Lisa gave you about she and I getting back together. It has surprised me too! We had become friends over recent years, but neither she nor I expected the ignition of the spark between us that happened. Perhaps it was because we were both at a low ebb in our lives at the same time. Anyway, it happened. And it grew.

I realise that you might be feeling worried about the whole thing. After all, it's a big change. I just wanted to say that I feel 100% sure that we are doing the right thing. We have fallen in love again as older, wiser, people. Let me reassure you that I will do everything in my power to make your daughter and grandsons happy. For one thing it greatly increases Lisa's financial security, having us pool our resources. The boys are delighted that I've moved in. Once I've sold my flat we'll be in a position to buy a new house. It's win-win for us all.

I know you and I haven't seen much of each other in recent years – which is normal after couples split up – but I hope that going forward we'll meet up as a family. I would like that. Of course, I will be with Lisa all the time now so I can help a lot more with childcare duties. Lisa tells me that you have gone away again on holiday to Pembrokeshire. I do hope that you are enjoying it, and I wish you all the best in your retirement.

Best wishes, Simon

Well. The first response that came into my mind was that it was pompous. Then I read it again and decided that wasn't quite fair. I did think it was rather clumsy, but then he was probably feeling tentative, given our history. Looking back, there had been a lot of simmering underground tension between us when he, Lisa and baby Nathan had lived in my house. Plus the discontent between Simon and Lisa had been palpable, with sullen faces at the dining table and hissed interchanges coming from their room that I tried to ignore. When you add in that I was struggling – reeling, in fact – from John's abandonment of me for another woman a few months before Lisa and Simon came to live with me, it's clear that our household was a powder keg waiting to explode. Which it did, and Simon left. I stared out of the window towards the cloud-hugged horizon, not really seeing it. I could acknowledge now that all those years ago when Simon left Lisa it had reopened my own wounds, still fresh, from John leaving, and so I was probably more scathing with Simon than was called for.

Anyway. All that was a long time ago. I blinked and shook away

31

the pictures that were starting to form in my mind and focussed again on the email in front of me while the little boats in Lower Town continued to sit patiently waiting for the tide. I allowed myself to consider that Simon had taken the trouble to write. And he had pointed out that he would be around to look after the kids. Typically, I'd had the boys to stay overnight at my house about once a fortnight, but lately that had tended to be just Joe on his own. Now there was Simon back in the picture, this new girl Ellen whom Joe liked, and increasingly over the next year as he turned sixteen, Nathan to look after Joe. I wondered where that left me.

I sat back and pondered. I would of course keep up my contact with my grandsons, but maybe at present everybody needed some space to settle into the new circumstances. Should I therefore take a step back? I felt around that idea and its implications. Then I brought myself back to the present moment in this beautiful place and contemplated whether I wanted to have a shower before heading out to the local pub for something to eat. I would reply to Simon tomorrow.

***

The next day began clear, and the weather forecast was for a bright summer day, not too hot and with a bit of breeze. Perfect. I planned to spend my first day of this holiday walking through Cwm Gwaun, the secret valley that had captured my imagination. I say secret because it's off the radar for the average tourist. On a website I had researched it was described as 'one of the great surprises of Pembrokeshire' and 'mythical and ancient'. It sounded intriguing and my sort of place.

Immediately to the north of Cwm Gwaun my map had shown me the tempting prospect of Mynydd Carningli, which is referred to as Angel Mountain in English. I remembered this great hill catching my eye when I passed through the village of Newport on my trek along the coast path. It seemed to stand over the village as if protecting it, and the summit was divided into a ridge of jagged peaks which reminded me of a giant stegosaurus – you know, one of those dinosaurs with a jagged back. Then there is a whole history associated with Carningli, if you care to read about it. This small mountain has always been associated with spirituality and angels, and it was where Saint Brynach used to go to find peace and refreshment hundreds of years ago. I had smiled as I read the legend which says that if you spend a night on Carningli, the next day either you would be mad or a poet. I hoped I was already on my way to being the latter.

My trusty map indicated that I could access Carningli along a footpath from the eastern end of Cwm Gwaun. Today I had planned to walk along the valley from west to east so it was a no-brainer to tack the climb up to the summit onto my river route. So, having stoked up on a gargantuan breakfast of fruit, bacon and egg with all the trimmings, toast and marmalade, and lashings of coffee, I got into my comfy old walking kit and loaded plenty of water into my backpack, along with the other things I always carry like a first aid pack, whistle, various medications, a compass (you never know), emergency food (nuts and seeds) and spare laces. Usually I carry rainwear and maybe other clothing, but today there wasn't a hint of rain on the forecast so I just took a light extra top. The final preparation was to slap on lots of sunscreen and pick up my sunglasses. I was bubbling with excitement as I went to the local shop to buy a picnic. While I was certainly full up after my breakfast, it was going to be a complete day's walking with nowhere to buy anything, so I needed to make sure I was supplied. I've done this before.

I took the car and descended the first few miles into the valley, where the map showed me there was somewhere to park. I found it easily, and I was the only person there. I got out of the car and was immediately immersed in the sense of the steep valley sides sheathing me in lush abundance. The only sounds were birdsong, the trickling of the River Gwaun and the occasional sheep. I laced up my boots and set off along the tiny lane in the valley bottom. As I proceeded along the winding route I saw a handful of cottages, a pub, a chapel and a school, which made up the buildings in this very long village. But the main features were the ubiquitous river and the thickly wooded slopes. The deepness of the green which led to the feeling of being immersed in it, was due to the fact that the trees were so densely packed. At least, that was the prosaic reason.

Eventually I came to the place where the lane swung round to the right and the valley became blurred and less steep. This was my cue to look for a bridle path on the left which would lift me from the valley bottom up the slopes of Carningli. It wasn't difficult to spot, and I set off through the woods, climbing all the time. Then the landscape unwrapped itself from woodland and I was in open country. I had my map to guide me, but it really wasn't necessary because all I had to do was to keep going up and up this small mountain.

The route I had chosen wasn't too steep, and I plugged onwards and upwards, pausing now and then to look back and appreciate how the gash of the valley was receding behind me. Rocky outcrops were ahead of me as I ascended, and I knew I wasn't far off the summit of Carningli. My raised heartbeat told not only of the hard physical work of the climb but also of my excitement and awe as I approached my goal.

Then the climb flattened out and I was on Carningli Common, right next to the rocky peaks that made up the summit. And the view! Now that I was at the top I could see ahead of me how the mountain swept down to the sea at the village of Newport. The terrain spread out like a giant map; between the village and the rearing headland of Dinas next to Pwllgwaelod (where I had encountered Benton and his mistress) were a couple of little bays cut into the coastline. I knew them. They were already my own country, because I had trekked through them when I had been on the Coast Path.

I turned round again to see the fold of the valley, with other mountains beyond it. I held my arms wide and spun slowly round and round, juxtaposing the twin views of countryside and coast, valley and sea, the sky a wide open dome of blue embracing it all.

My breath hissed through my teeth. I knew now for myself why Carningli was considered mystical and why saints and a long succession of others had always come here for spiritual refreshment. This mountain was both further beyond and also between; between the sea and the valley and the sky. Perhaps also between one world and another?

Carningli

Between the sea, the valley and the sky,
Here on Carningli, this enchanted hill
So mountain-like in occult power to fill
The mind with thoughts unknown, I dream how my
Before-and-after lives, spread map-wise, lie
As if new-shaped and contoured by the will
To make it over, all my life until
The zigzag climb that brought me heaven-high
To point my future path. And there's Cwm Gwaun,
Thick-wooded, shadow-strewn, a gash cut deep
Beneath this spellbound vantage-point of mine -
That road I'd walked like one whose restless sleep
Or breathless last few steps at last combine
To spring Carningli's soul-awakening sweep.

My first Pembrokeshire poem.

Chapter 5

Halfway through my holiday already. Where had the time gone? Every day was full of the discovery of new little gems in this beautiful county. I had just messaged Cameron and was now skimming idly through my Facebook newsfeed while I sat outside the café in the sunshine, feeling grateful for its warmth on my face. I kept glancing along the street. Would I recognise Barbara without Benton?

Yes, I had eventually decided to make contact with the nice lady from Pwllgwaelod and we were now on first name terms. I had messaged her and said I was staying in Fishguard and enquired in a nonchalant way if the cottage she had mentioned was being rented out yet. She replied that she would find out and asked if I fancied having a cup of coffee while I was here. Why not, I thought.

A cottage, sleeps two, she had said. Since I had been back in Pembrokeshire this cottage had taken root in my imagination. For the current trip, my boutique hotel was working well. But if – I mean when – I come back I would want more of my own space where I could think and write. My poetry was starting to germinate and to push its way out of me, in this place of beauty where I was free from distractions. And, on a more banal note, a big cooked breakfast was more than I could handle on a daily basis. The imagined cottage had painted itself into my thoughts. There it was, built of the local stone, with a small red door and symmetrical windows on either side of it plus two windows upstairs. Like Joe would have drawn a house when he was about three. Smoke curled out of the chimney in the thatched roof and there was a winding path through a verdant front garden and a cat on the step. In fact it was the cottage from every fairy tale I had ever read.

'It's Rhian, isn't it?' It was just as well that Barbara recognised me, because she was hidden under a big floppy hat and sunglasses, so I could well have let her pass me by. She was also tidily attired in a flowery dress with a cardigan over her arm; rather different to her walking clothes. I had chosen smart casual too. We shook hands, slightly awkwardly on my part, while Barbara sat down and took her sunglasses off, which was always better for conversation, I thought.

'I say, fancy you getting in touch with me. I was so pleased to hear from you! Where are you staying in Fishguard? Are you enjoying your holiday? Are you doing some walking?' She was just as smiley, enthusiastic and slightly manic as I had remembered. We ordered our cappuccinos and in no time Barbara had extracted from me where I was staying, the places I'd been and even a broad outline of my backstory. It wasn't that she was nosy, exactly; she seemed genuinely interested in people. By the time we were on to our second coffees and a slice of cake, I'd also managed to discover that she and her husband had retired to Pembrokeshire a few years ago and that she had sons and grandchildren back in England. She was impressed to hear that I had been drawn to Cwm Gwaun and from there I had climbed up Carningli.

'Yes, Carningli is a rather special place, isn't it?' she said. 'Do you know the legend about if you stay there overnight you come down mad or a poet?'

I told her that I did, and that I was tentatively attracted to the idea as an adventure, but I didn't feel brave enough to camp out there on my own. I didn't mention my own aspirations as a poet.

'My son is coming to stay in early September. He's experienced in leading expeditions – he's got tents, sleeping bags and everything. He'd be happy to stay with you up there. Perhaps I could come too! Oh, that would be fun! Is there any chance you would be back in September?'

That was my cue. 'Well, you had mentioned a cottage that was going to be available soon for renting. Maybe that would be ready in September?'

'Ah yes. That cottage. I forget its name, but I know it's something pretty in Welsh. It's owned by a friend of mine – well, just an acquaintance really – she's a friend of a friend. Anyway, this cottage was left to her after someone died. I'm a bit vague about the exact story, but that's what happened, apparently. She's out of the country at the moment, but my friend had her number so I was able to contact her.'

I waited, containing my impatience during the rambling delivery, while Barbara fumbled in her bag for her phone. And then she had to get her reading glasses on to see the screen. 'Here we are,' she said at last, and read out the message. *There's just a few things to finish. The cottage won't be ready to rent out properly until the end of the summer, although at the moment I have some friends of friends staying there.* 'Then there was another message later, detailing the company that's going to be handling the letting, and also the address… hang on a minute…' She scrolled through, muttering under her breath. 'Ah yes, here it is. Shall I forward it to you?'

And there it was on my screen. I had the actual address, which meant nothing to me at present. Barbara explained that it was in the no-man's land between Fishguard and Newport and gave me complex instructions on how to find it. I nodded politely, but what I really wanted to do was to put the postcode into my maps app. When I did that I got the location straightaway. It existed. It was real.

***

I parked the car at a pub, which was called The Harp, and set off on foot, my phone map at the ready. The straggle of houses thinned out as I walked down the quiet road. Then a turn to the right, down a single-track lane. This was the correct place, my map told me; it should be just about here. I started to feel panic rising. Where was it? Surely this wasn't all some elaborate hoax? Then I realised I was just outside the place. The name, Heddfan, was painted in wobbly letters on a stone which was propped up by the front door –

not particularly eye-catching unless you were looking for it.

I suppose the cottage must have been constructed of stone – I don't know much about these things – but it was also covered with a white rendering of some sort. It was single storey, and it had a tiled roof, not a thatched one, and a chimney. The front door, which was painted dark green, wasn't in the centre of the cottage; there were two windows to one side of the door, and one window to the other. There was a lean-to outhouse with a murky small window tacked on to one end of the structure. I stood at the front gate and took it all in, gradually rejigging my fantasy cottage to correspond with the reality before my eyes. Well, the front door and windows were similar to my imaginings, but the shape of the building itself, with what seemed to be three rooms in a row and an outhouse, struck me as being elongated. Then it occurred to me: was this what was known as a Welsh longhouse? I had read a bit about these dwellings, which had originally been constructed for livestock at one end and people at the other. Wow. How romantic, if that's what it had been. My imaginary cottage was speedily getting ditched in favour of this authentic version.

There was a straggle of greenery and rampant plants in the front garden, just inside a low wall, and an open space at the side. This space was big enough for a car and, judging from the tyre marks, there had been one there recently. I stepped up to the front door and knocked quite gently with the creaky brass knocker. I didn't have a clue what I was going to say if someone should answer it. However, no-one seemed to be at home, so after checking over my shoulder for lurking onlookers I went to the first window and peeped in. It turned out to be the kitchen. I was pleasantly surprised to see that the facilities in there didn't match the archaic exterior of the cottage; the kitchen was a modern – well, fairly modern – set-up complete with cooker, fridge and what looked like an old central heating boiler. A few used plates and cutlery were sitting on the worktop. Then my eyes were drawn to a table and, more particularly the laptop that was on it. Since the rest of the room might have been taken from the sixties, the computer looked glaringly out of place. On the other hand, surely that would mean there was wi-fi? Old-fashioned is all very charming, but give me internet and a good phone signal, please. Immediately I checked my phone. The signal was strong enough.

I tore myself away from that window to look in another window, on the other side of the front door, which presented me with a view of a cosy sitting room featuring a worn but comfy-looking sofa, a fireplace corresponding to the chimney I'd seen, two faded armchairs, a small Welsh dresser, a low table strewn with used wine glasses and plates littered with crumbs. I also noted there was a radiator. The final room that I peeped into, next to the sitting room, was the bedroom. Here I didn't linger because rumpled sheets from the double bed, plus toiletries and clothing, were scattered everywhere, and it would have seemed indecent if I were to be caught gawping at such an intimate scene. Even though I knew I shouldn't, I couldn't resist going quickly round to the rear of the dwelling where there was a conservatory-type passage along the back of the house connecting the bedroom to what presumably had to be a small bathroom that had been added behind the kitchen. I could look in through the large windows of the conservatory-passage down the stone-flagged hallway to the front door. There were doors leading from this hallway to the kitchen and the sitting room. I didn't want to loiter behind the house, so with a quick look at the back garden (there were fattening apples on a tree) I went out of the property again and stood in the lane, committing it all to memory. I wondered if the couple staying there could be on honeymoon.

***

The man behind the bar in The Harp wished me a cheery 'good afternoon' as I went into the comfortable Lounge. I sat down with my half of lager. I didn't take too much notice of what was around me, because my mind was saturated with impressions of the cottage. I went over my recollections of the layout and what I'd seen in each room. I could pretty much reconstruct it all in my head, although I realised there were some details I hadn't taken in.

For instance, was there a radiator in the bedroom? In the passageway? Surely you wouldn't have a boiler to run one radiator. So I persuaded myself that there must be radiators in every room and readjusted the picture in my head.

I brought my thoughts back from the cottage and picked up the menu to choose something for lunch. It was a typical pub menu with all the favourites on it – sausage and mash, gammon and chips, steak pie, filled jacket potatoes and the rest. Then my eye was caught by the specials on the blackboard and my choice was made. Lamb cawl, served in the traditional way with bread and cheese.

Auntie used to make cawl sometimes when we went to her house in Carmarthen. She made the bestest cawl. Mam never made it. She said people didn't eat it in Cardiff. Auntie would put the big pot on the table and put the cawl into our dishes with a big spoon, much bigger than you could put into your mouth. Like a giant's spoon. It would be all steamy and Mam told me to blow on each little piece of lamb before I put it in my mouth. And there were pieces of carrot and lots of leeks, which tasted sweet, and some green stuff, but I don't know the name of that. The biggest bits were the potatoes, and I had to cut them up with my spoon. Or Mam would help me. The boys used to gobble it down quick and ask for more, but I was as full as full could be after my bowl, and the bread and the cheese too...

I was jolted back to the present when the barman asked what he could get me. 'On holiday, is it?' he asked, eager to be pleasant. My accent is a sure give-away.

I replied that I was. I hesitated while he passed my order through to the kitchen. Then I said, 'Do you know a cottage about ten minutes' walk from here, towards the coast? It's called Heddfan.'

He frowned. 'Not sure. Hang on, Idris will know, I expect. Idris!' He called out to a silver-haired man who was sitting with a glass of ale and a whisky chaser, his empty lunch plate also on the

41

table. The man put down his newspaper and I saw he was dressed in a light jacket and a scarlet bow tie, of all things. I also noticed a straw Panama hat and a walking cane on the seat next to him. Perhaps he'd stepped straight out of a barbershop quartet.

'Heddfan? Let me see. That's further down the lane than my house. I do believe it's been renovated since the old lady died. I expect it's going to be sold, but I don't know.' His voice was distinctive; mellifluous and cultured were the words that sprang to my mind.

'Ah. Only this young lady was asking, see.'

Young lady indeed. Still, a bit of flattery didn't hurt.

'Are you interested in buying the place, my dear?' said Idris.

'Oh no, not at all. I'd heard it might be available as a rental property soon, a holiday let, and I thought while I was in the area I'd check it out. Just out of interest, you know.' My innate resistance to revealing myself too much to strangers kicked in.

'Ah, a pity. I thought I might be going to get a charming neighbour.' He smiled courteously, which served to take any potential creepiness out of his gallant remark. 'I live next door to that cottage, you see. You might have noticed a large house set back from the road, covered with ivy. In need of a bit of repair, to tell the truth.'

A genial gentleman. But I didn't really want to start sharing my life story with him. I told him I could vaguely recollect a house that was probably his, by which time my lunch had arrived, so I didn't have to engage further with him. Still, he was pleasant enough.

Before I left, I used the online Welsh-English dictionary on my phone to look up 'Heddfan'. It translated as 'peaceful place'.

***

The office for the company renting cottages in West Wales was in Haverfordwest, so I thought I might as well call in the next day, after I had had a chance to sleep on my impressions. I found the place easily enough. I explained my mission to the woman who was working in the office, namely that I wanted to know when

42

Heddfan was available. I said that I was interested in a long-term rent.

She frowned over her computer screen. 'Ah yes, we're expecting to start advertising it from September. Were you thinking of booking for a month?'

'I'm thinking of a year,' I said.

Chapter 6

I turned the car into my drive and switched the engine off. I didn't get out straight away because I was trying to tether my emotions. After a few minutes I collected myself and went into my house. There was still post on the mat because nowadays the postman must have changed his round and he didn't come until mid-afternoon. I switched the light on. My hall, decorated in dark green which had seemed a good idea at the time, could be a bit gloomy, and at nine o'clock on an evening in early August the sky was just starting to dim. I put my keys and bag down and plugged the kettle in – an automatic routine upon coming back home. I glanced at my day's mail and discovered that all three letters were junk. No surprise there.

I settled myself down with a cup of tea in my favourite chair in the living room, which had a view of the back garden through the patio doors. A blackbird was hopping around looking hopefully for worms, no doubt. I love my garden birds. I expect that the garden at Heddfan will be alive with wildlife. My lawn and borders were looking neat, because the gardener had been while I was away. Note to self – I must arrange to keep him on while I'm away. There will be so much to sort out, and not long to do it.

The afternoon and evening had not gone as I would have thought. If I'm honest, I had been dreading telling Lisa of my plan to have a year away in West Wales, even though I had taken pains to point out straightaway that I would be coming back every month or so, when I would see her and the boys. Of course, she was surprised – it's not the sort of thing you expect to hear – but the out-and-out battle that I had been expecting didn't happen. She had called out to Simon who was lying low in the kitchen or somewhere, 'Hey Simon, guess what my mother's planning to do!'

Simon emerged, looking suitably eager and appeasing. I had sent a conciliatory and pleasant reply to his email, but I could see he was unsure of how he should behave, even though this was his home now, as well as Lisa's. Apparently he had moved all his possessions in, and his flat was for sale. Simon was a tall, good-looking bloke, fit from all the cycling he did. 'What are you planning, Rhian?' His smile was only slightly forced.

'She's only going to be a recluse in the wild west for a year to write her poetry,' burst out Lisa before I could reply. 'If you can manage that long,' she added to me. After I had clarified that it was Pembrokeshire we were talking about, not cowboy country, I explained patiently that this was an adventure for me, and that many people who retired early took the opportunity to do something completely different, something challenging.

'OK, I get that. But there are lots of different things you could do without hiding yourself away,' said Lisa.

'That's true for many other people. But what appeals to me is this cottage in a beautiful place where I can really settle down to concentrate on poetry for a long period of time. And I will be coming back now and again.'

'You mean it's a writer's retreat?' said Simon. 'That seems really worthwhile. And brave, may I add. Lots of famous writers work in a retreat setting. Look at Dylan Thomas and his boathouse, for example.' To be fair, the man was really trying.

Nathan was sitting on the floor, glued to his phone. I didn't even know he was listening to the conversation, but without taking his eyes from the screen he said, 'Wicked, Gran. Go for it.' Joe was next to him, playing with his cars and oblivious to the swirl of adult conversation above his head.

Lisa held up her hands. 'Alright, alright.' She turned to me and bowed formally. 'Mum, I wish you good luck with your writer's retreat in West Wales.'

I felt as if I was being mocked, and I didn't care for it. But it was better than having a row, so I made an effort and let it go. I perched on the floor beside Joe to admire his little fleet of cars. I could see that the beige carpet was getting threadbare and grubby when I was closer to it like this. I checked my first impulse to offer to help buy a replacement. That was Simon's territory now. He had moved along the sofa to sit closer to Lisa. He felt for her hand and whispered something in her ear. She looked at him and they both held each other's eyes and smiled, enclosed together in the secret. They really have fallen in love again, I thought. I just hope it lasts.

'How's work going, Simon?' I said.

He looked startled by the direct question, but quite pleased that I was asking it. We all chatted amicably for a while, and the conversation billowed back and forth. Then Lisa said, 'So what's this cottage like, then? How many bedrooms? Does it have a view of the sea?'

What to tell her? 'It's a typical Welsh cottage in style,' I said. 'It's stone built and cosy, with a nice little garden. It only has one bedroom, but that's all I need. And it doesn't have a sea view, although it's only about a mile from the coast.' She asked if I had photographs, and I had to tell her I didn't. Publicity for the place hadn't yet been up on the internet. I described it some more in the most glowing terms I could muster and stressed how its authenticity and charm had been retained, despite a refurbishment to modern standards. I sounded like I was a bad estate agent selling the place, and I grew more uncomfortable by the minute.

'Is the bathroom modern? With a proper shower?'

I looked her in the eye. I might as well get it over with. 'I haven't actually seen the bathroom. In fact, I haven't been inside the property at all. But I have had a good look through all the windows. Except the bathroom.'

That's when all hell broke loose. Lisa didn't mince her words when she demanded an explanation for the fact that I, a supposedly intelligent woman, should agree to rent a place for a year, a whole year, without setting foot inside it. How could I explain to her how I had felt, how the area and the cottage, the 'peaceful place', spoke to me? You just know when something is right, I had said, but my limp justification didn't cut much ice with Lisa.

The menfolk had all found something to do in other rooms, and I can't say I blamed them. What about the terms of the Rental Agreement? Have you signed anything yet or can you still back out? She fired the questions at me, and my self-control was starting to evaporate. I told her that the contract was for three months, renewable up until a year, and I had already paid a deposit.

I gathered my resources. 'Lisa, this is what I want to do, and it will be fine. I know you're just worried for me, but I really can lead my own life. What's the worst that can happen? If it doesn't work out I'll come home after the first three months, or before that if I really needed to, and I'd just have to lose the money. Honestly, you don't need to be so concerned.'

She put up a few more objections, but basically my steady refusal to be bullied had won the day. We made one of our trademark uneasy truces. The thing was, in a little corner of my mind I knew she had a point. It was a bit crazy to be renting a place when you hadn't properly inspected it. I was trusting my gut on this one. What was taking early retirement for if you couldn't do something a bit mad?

It took me most of my drive home and a good bit of deep breathing to calm myself down to anything like a normal level. Yes, I had kept my cool, but it had been an effort. Still, she hadn't freaked out at the main idea of me taking myself off for a year, which is what I had been dreading. She was OK about me not being on hand for that length of time, even if she was dubious and somewhat scathing about the cottage and my arrangements. I let out a long, slow breath. That hurdle was over.

Now all I had to do was tell Cameron.

***

When I had got home from Pembrokeshire, top of my to-do list was to see Lisa and to see Cameron. I hadn't wanted to tell either of them on the phone what my plans were. Then I had wimped out of the difficult meeting that I needed to have with Cameron, and I wrote him a long explanatory email instead which I ended up not sending. Whereas it cleared my head to put all my thoughts down logically in writing, my conscience nagged me that this really was a cop-out and a cowardly thing to do, given there was so much I had to say and I wanted to let him down as gently as I could. So it was back to plan A and I arranged to go round to his place.

I had never had to do this before. There had been several relationships over the past few years, but they had either been short term or they had just run their course after a few weeks or months and so petered out naturally. There had never been any upset involved, which was not like when John announced that he loved someone else and he was leaving me to be with her. That had been a profound shock, coming after more than twenty years of marriage. But it was all a long time ago.

No, I've never actually taken the step of ending a relationship. Cameron and I had worked well together for the last year or so, when we were both professional individuals. It was convenient for two busy people. Now I had chosen to leave the professional part of me behind, and I could feel a gap starting to insinuate itself between us. Did I love him? We'd never taken the step of saying the L-word, and I acknowledged that it had never really been a romance. And now I was going away for a whole year, and it wasn't fair to expect Cameron to twiddle his thumbs waiting for me to come back every few weeks. Even though I was not looking forward to actually having the conversation with him, finishing it was the honourable thing to do.

Cameron's flat was ten floors up and that's about how many seconds it took to glide up to it in the lift. You felt you had hardly left the ground and there you were. The lift doors whispered open for me and my footsteps were similarly soundless as I trod on the carpet leading up to his door, along the inscrutable corridor of separate entrances which all harboured their secrets and isolated lives. I'd never had any hankering to live in a flat, even though the view from a high floor like this could be pretty stunning. I preferred to be able to step out onto my sweet grass and look for the blackbird.

I rang the doorbell. Funny, we had never got round to having keys for each other's home. 'Hello, stranger,' said Cameron, smiling, and stepped back to allow me in. He kissed me on the cheek, smelling of the piquant aftershave that he used and, as usual, he was dressed immaculately, this time in shirt and trousers. He led me into the living area and sat down beside me on the white leather sofa.

'I could really do with a drink,' I said truthfully. 'Gin and tonic would be nice. Not too big, though.'

'So I gather your trip was good?' he said from the other side of the kitchen counter where he was popping ice cubes out of the tray and slicing the lemon. You got the full works at Cameron's.

I told him that it was. He passed me my drink and sat down on the sofa opposite to mine this time. We clinked glasses and wished each other good health, like we always did. The gin and tonic was strong, and I realised I would have to take it slowly, because I would be driving home later rather than staying overnight like I usually did. I put my drink down on the polished coffee table between us and started to speak at the same moment that he did. We both stopped and laughed in embarrassment, insisting that the other go first. Cameron said, 'There's something I have to tell you, so I'll go first if you don't mind.' He crossed his legs and jiggled his foot up and down; a most un-Cameron-like movement.

Various disaster scenarios flashed through my mind in those few seconds before he spoke again – illness, crime, family in trouble. What I wasn't ready for was him saying, 'I think you and I should stop seeing each other. We've been drifting a bit lately, don't you think? Since you retired you seem mainly concerned with dashing off to Pembrokeshire. You've changed, Rhian.'

Talk about wrong-footed. I just stared open-mouthed, while my brain tried to process this turn of events. In my peripheral vision I noticed a plane flying by, in the distance. It reminded me of how high up we were. I wonder where they're heading for, I thought.

Cameron sat forward in his seat and linked his hands before he continued. He gripped his hands so tightly his knuckles were nearly white. 'I don't want to hurt you, but we don't spend as much time together or have as much fun as we used to. We seem to have different goals and aspirations now, and life's too short to spend more of it together if we're past our best. Do you understand?'

Oh yes, I understood alright. He had practically stolen my script. This wasn't how it was supposed to be, but actually, wasn't it easier than me being the one doing the dumping? 'Yes,' I said, matching his business-like manner. 'I get it, and I think you're right. Thank you for your honesty. In fact, I am planning to spend more time in Pembrokeshire to concentrate on my writing.' After his revelation, I didn't feel like disclosing the details of my exodus for a year and subjecting myself to his incredulity about the whole venture. Especially after my experience with Lisa.

We both took a gulp of our drinks and eyed each other. Was that it, as simple and civilised as that? Now what happens, I thought. Do I just wish him all the best for the future and go? He sat back and laughed, and I recognised it as relief. 'I've been dreading telling you. Breaking up is never easy, as they say. Oh, and there's just one more thing.' He drained his glass in one gulp and the ice cubes chinked against the side. I waited. He looked down and rubbed his finger along an invisible mark on the sofa arm.

'When you were away the first time, I bumped into someone at the gym who I vaguely knew. She was an ex-colleague. I saw her again while you were away again this time and we got chatting, as you do, and ended up having a drink. The upshot was we decided to go running together. We've done that twice so far.'

I said nothing because I didn't know what I was supposed to say.

'I'm only telling you this in case someone has seen us and says something.'

'Why should I care if you train with someone, especially not now. Are you going out with her?' I didn't see why I should beat about the bush.

He could hardly have looked more uncomfortable. 'No, not exactly. But that is a possibility now you and I… you know, now that you and I are over.'

I didn't push him regarding 'not exactly'. I didn't want us to end on a sour note, so I left it there.

I went to the bathroom before I left. As I washed my hands, I saw tucked at the back of the shelf a pack of make-up cleansing pads. I picked them up and examined them. They weren't mine.

***

There were three keys: one for the front door, one for the back door and one for the little lean-to building on the side. They were linked together by a keyring which had a leather fob with a Welsh dragon motif on it. They felt solid in my hand as I left the heavily laden car and went up to the front door. Now that I was here, I hardly dared to go in. I fumbled to get the correct key and door swung open. There was a doormat so I automatically wiped my feet before I crossed the threshold. The hall was flagged with proper old-fashioned stone tiles. I hadn't noticed them before. Which room should I go in first?

I chose the kitchen. There was a fresh smell of the cleaning that had obviously taken place quite recently, a plant on the table, and a handbook of information which I would peruse later, and a welcome pack including teas and Welsh cakes. I turned around slowly and viewed everything – all a bit dated but perfectly serviceable. It was a cottage after all, what could you expect? The living room was next. It was just how I had remembered from when I had peered in through the window. Then it was as if I had been viewing a painting, but now I had stepped through the frame and into that painting. I was part of it. Was I through the Looking Glass? I didn't linger to try the sofa – that would come later. Instead, I went down the corridor and into the bedroom. This room looked rather different from what I had seen, now that the bed was tidily made with matching floral duvet cover and pillowcases, and no clothes strewn over the floor. Now I was able to take in the old-fashioned wardrobe and dressing table, fortunately made from a light wood so they weren't too imposing in the small room.

I went down the conservatory-type corridor where three doors confronted me: one to the bathroom, one out to the garden and one to the lean-to. I held my breath as I pushed open the bathroom door because this was the only room I hadn't seen. I needn't have worried; it passed the test. Like the kitchen, it was a bit out of date, with a shower over the bath and a toilet with a chain, but it was enough to suit my needs. I ran both the shower and the tap in the washbasin and allowed the hot water that gushed out to play over my hand. What on earth would Lisa have said if the bathroom had let the property down?

Finally, I went in the antiquated outhouse and to my surprise, there was a washing machine along with an ironing board, vacuum cleaner, and a few other bits and pieces. Obviously, a forerunner to a modern utility room. I realised that I had never even missed the presence of a washing machine when I had looked in through the window, so this find was a bonus.

And that was it. The preliminary tour was completed, and there were no obvious flaws. I was safely within my temporary home. I sat down at the kitchen table and found I was shaking.

Chapter 7

Two weeks in and my occupancy had started to crystallise into a flexible routine – to excuse the oxymoron – consisting of walking, exploring, enjoying the peace, reading, writing and settling in. The unpacking had taken a couple of days, along with filling the fridge and cupboards after a trip to the Co-op in Fishguard. I had felt comfortable in the bed right from the start, and the sofa welcomed me into its embrace as if it had been made for me. I should in fairness list anything that didn't get ten out of ten. The TV was small and didn't get many channels (I'm a bit of a BBC girl anyway, so it didn't matter), the cooker was inefficient (but I didn't intend to cook elaborate meals) and the internet signal was only tolerably strong. However, this was offset by a robust phone signal. Don't ask me how that works; I was just glad to have it. I had tentatively tried the radiators and they had obliged by pumping out some heat, although it would have to wait until colder weather descended before they could really be put to the test.

Talking of weather, the early autumn was gently starting to touch the leaves and it was noticeable that the evenings were drawing in. I had been in touch with Barbara, who was ecstatic that I was in the area, and we arranged to meet up. Apparently, her son wasn't coming to visit this September, so I was off the hook about the mooted trip up CarnIngli to spend the night.

I was modestly pleased with my progress on the poetry front and was taking my time to explore different verse forms. I was particularly attracted by the idea of conforming my words and rhymes to fixed schemes. There were many such rhyme schemes, such as the sonnet, rondel or ballade, and it intrigued me that these disciplines existed and that I could bend my words to fit their particular rules. But far from inhibiting my thoughts and output, it seemed to enhance them. I had read some villanelles, where only two rhymes are allowed and two lines are repeated as a sort of refrain. I found I loved the music of that.

So I played around with my thoughts and let the interworld mood that had suffused me take shape tentatively on the page. It took me several hours of wrestling with this difficult task, but I had eventually produced something that I was satisfied with. It was for this that I had come to Heddfan.

Liminal

The windows give you back that wishful gaze.
Too painterly, the cottage of your dreams!
Step through the canvas, end the mirror-phase.

What if the past life imaged

My endeavours were interrupted by a single knock on the front door. It was the first time I'd heard it and initially I wondered what it was. Straightaway I recognised on the doorstep the dapper elderly gentleman with whom I had talked briefly in The Harp in August. The bow tie, a blue one today, was a potent reminder. He lifted his hat to greet me. 'Ah, good morning. It's my beautiful new neighbour. I'd perceived that the house was now occupied, so I thought I would bring you this floral tribute to welcome you to the neighbourhood.' With that, he proffered me a trailing bunch of wildflowers. I can't say I knew the names of any of them, but all the colours made a wonderful wild bouquet, and what woman doesn't like to receive flowers?

I stammered my thanks, quite inarticulate because I was so surprised. He beamed and turned to go. I made a split-second decision. 'Do you want to come in and have something to drink?'

He accepted with a formal bow. I showed him into the living room and swept away my plethora of books, paper and other paraphernalia so he could sit down on the sofa, while I took the armchair. It was messy, but my excuse was I hadn't long moved in and I wasn't expecting visitors. While the kettle was boiling (thank goodness it was an electric one) I struggled to remember what the barman had called him. It was a Welsh name. Ifor? Something like that. I was close. It was Idris, I discovered.

Idris had forgotten that I was renting Heddfan; he assumed I had bought it. 'But welcome anyway. It's always a joy to give flowers to a lady, and we are going to be neighbours for the next year, after all. What brings you to our humble village?' It seemed that 'minding your own business' was an unknown concept around here. I decided to go with it. So I went through the whole rigmarole about retiring early, having some spare money from my lump sum, abundant free time, no ties and loving the area, but I didn't mention my writing aspirations. I wanted to keep that to myself.

We talked about the village. It wasn't a typical village layout because it had a main road running through the edge of it, but it had the necessary ingredients, namely two pubs, a grocery shop with post office, a school, and a church. Because of its proximity to the main A road between Fishguard and Cardigan, it also had a garage. Then it was only a mile downhill to the local beach, Pwllgwaelod. Idris assured me that it was a pleasant place to live, and that The Harp was the beating heart of the village.

'With a name like Rhian, do you have some Welsh ties?'

'Yes, I was born and brought up in Cardiff to Welsh parents, then I moved away to university and never looked back. Until now, that is.'

He clapped his hands. 'That's astonishing! It sounds amazingly similar to my own story. What a divine coincidence! I too was born in Wales – hence my name – then I was seduced by the lure of the bright lights in London and made my home there. Publishing and books were my game.' He looked around the sitting room and rested his gaze where I had arranged my books on the welcoming shelves of the Welsh dresser. That was apart from those that were spilled around my feet and had erupted onto the sofa. 'You are a reader, I see.' He picked up a volume, which was entitled *How Poetry Works*. 'Ah, I know this book. It's a little gem, in my opinion. Do we have a budding poet in our midst? How delicious!'

I drew back. No, I couldn't expose myself. Not yet. Maybe not ever. Hedgehog-like, I curled inwards. 'I'm just dabbling,' I said, and firmly turned the conversation back to him. 'What made you move from London to here?'

'When retirement came around, we decided to make the break and live somewhere as unlike London as possible. We'd had enough of the whole treadmill of big city life. So we ended up here and it was the best thing we ever did.'

I didn't ask who 'we' referred to. I was still a novice at learning the upfront habits of the friendly locals. 'And yours is the big house next door, I believe?'

'It is, for my sins. It could do with a lick of paint and a few repairs now, but it's been home for the last fifteen years and I expect it to continue to be so for the rest of my life. I would be honoured if you would come and have tea with me some time.'

I hesitated only briefly before I accepted his invitation. I had taken an unaccountable liking to Idris. Certainly he was quirky and eccentric, yet I sensed a warmth and lightness about him. After spending my working life with predictable and driven businesspeople he was diverting and felt like a breath of fresh air to kick off my sabbatical year. Also, I was sure he was as unthreatening as a tea cosy. So we set a date for a few days' time.

'Splendid! I'll ask Sharon to make scones,' he said.

*****

Hi Lisa

Glad you liked the pictures I sent and hope you could see for yourself how snug and quite idyllic Heddfan is. It was nice to talk to you all on a video call and to have walked you round my new domain, but I wanted you also to have some stills to look back on.

56

It was lovely to engage with the boys too, although I get it that they don't want to talk to me much. TBH I was grateful that Joe wanted to acknowledge me at all!

Lisa, I've really fallen on my feet here. It's only about a quarter of a mile to the facilities of the village (pub, shop, garage) and a mile from the little beach that I sent the pic of. The wifi and phone signal are pretty good. As I've said, I'm lucky to have found the place. I'm feeling just about settled in now, and the weather is being really kind.

The days are passing very pleasantly. I've made a start on studying poetry and poetics and trying my hand at producing my own work. And I've met my neighbour. In fact I've been invited there for afternoon tea – today, as it happens. I've also been to the pub and it's nice and friendly – a real 'local'.

How's the house hunting going? I'm glad that you're going to stay in the same area, so that the boys won't have to change schools. I was amazed by how quickly Simon's flat sold.

I read back what I had written so far and sighed. It was hard to hit the right note, and my words seemed to smack of defensiveness. Or was that just me? I wanted to really sell my new accommodation to Lisa, and to convince her that I had made the right decision to come here. I hoped she wouldn't get on my case again. Perhaps the photographs that I had sent would help. I had spent considerable time taking them, getting the best angles and the best lighting – real estate agent stuff. Why do we seek the approval of our grown-up children?

I finished the email with a few more gushing comments and signed off. Lisa always seemed rushed and distracted when I phoned or video messaged her, so I thought an email might be more useful. Anyway, she had her own life, enriched now by Simon's reappearance in it, so why should I be concerned about what she thought? I made a determined effort to distract my thoughts, and turned again to my latest poem, which still progressing slowly. I knew I was making it more challenging for myself by choosing a formal structure, but that was what appealed;

virtually anyone could generate free verse, but something like a villanelle required the discipline and thoughtfulness of rhyme, only two rhyme sounds in the whole poem, in fact. Gaze, phase, glaze, pays, amaze, ways... dreams, regimes, schemes, beams. How many more rhymes would I be able to persuade into my words to keep the momentum going? Praise, days, delays, stays... themes, seems, deems. *Step through the canvas, end the mirror phase.* The original spark for the poem had been struck by my view of the cottage interior from the outside, but then it had harnessed its own message. I wondered if my attraction to formal verse had its basis in being comfortable with rigours and restrictions, which had a parallel throughout my career. An accountant is nothing if not constrained by the strict rules of numbers. But the blessed, magical difference here was that I chose the words to fit the form, from an abundance of options that danced and sparkled and teased, whereas numbers solidly obeyed their earthbound rules. I was done with numbers.

I sat back to contemplate these thoughts. Already in the short time I'd been here the little sitting room had gathered itself around me. I had settled on my own chosen corner of the sofa, shored up with cushions. There wasn't going to be time now to immerse myself in my work; I was due at Idris's house in half an hour. I decided to browse Facebook, which is always a useful way to waste a few minutes. My gaze slid over various friends, usually smiling at me from some bar or picturesque location. I hadn't posted anything yet from Heddfan and I probably wouldn't. This place was mine. Writers on retreat (I liked to think of myself in that way, since Simon had first mooted it) didn't go splashing their doings all over social media. I was just thinking that I should be logging off and getting changed into something suitable for my afternoon tea appointment, when who should pop up on the screen but Cameron. There he was, with his arm slung around the woman's shoulders, their matching smiles gleaming.

I looked long and hard. So this was my replacement. She looked a few years younger than me, this petite, sporty blonde. Bottle blonde, no doubt. As I had been, until I took the plunge to start revealing the real me – my grey hair – a couple of months before I left work. I carefully probed my feeling about the woman, as you would gently examine a suspect tooth with your tongue. And I realised that, apart from normal feminine curiosity, I didn't actually care. It was all in the past now, and with every day that past was getting more and more remote. I unfriended Cameron, closed my laptop and went to the bedroom to get changed.

***

Idris's house stood foursquare and symmetrically windowed at the end of a drive, which was flanked by trees that were just beginning to yield to the advancing autumn. I didn't know what kind of trees they were, and if I was going to be a proper country dweller perhaps I should learn more about the natural world around me, rather than just rejoicing in it on a sensory level, like I did. A young man was cutting the grass, guiding his mower round the brimming flower beds. We waved and smiled at each other as I approached the front door.

There is nothing so incongruous as an electric doorbell on an old front door, and it seemed entirely more fitting that it was the sound of a big brass knocker that resounded sonorously through the house. Idris welcomed me in with a mock bow followed by a kiss on both cheeks. He smelled pleasant; you wouldn't say it was aftershave, more like an old-fashioned soap. He still wore his trademark bow tie, even though he was in his own home. Perhaps it was for his guest's benefit.

'Rhian, how delightful to see you. Let me take your jacket. My, what a fetching blouse that is.' He hung my jacket on the dark wooden hallstand, complete with a mirror in the centre panel. It had been some years since I'd seen one of those. In fact, we used to have one when I was a child. 'Let's sit in the drawing room, shall we?' He led the way into a room off the hall, which did not turn out to be quite as grand as its title. Nevertheless, it was a dignified, high-ceilinged space with the ubiquitous three-piece suite in maroon with gold braid trim plus matching footstools, coffee tables, a paisley-patterned carpet and a large fireplace. But the defining feature was the walls, in that they were mainly hidden by overflowing bookshelves. You could have referred to the room as a library, which to my mind was as sophisticated as calling it a drawing room.

'Do sit down and make yourself at home. Sharon, that's the kind soul who does for me, has put everything ready, so I'll just be two ticks bringing the tea in.' The central coffee table was already laden with a piled platter of scones, plus butter, jam and cream in little ceramic pots on the side. There were plates featuring floral patterns and there were real linen napkins, ironed and folded. I looked around the room and tried not very successfully to read titles on the spines of the books. There were several pictures of a couple on the mantlepiece, and I itched to get up and study them, but I didn't want to get caught being nosy.

Idris pushed open the door with his foot and entered carrying a giant tray bearing the teapot and other accoutrements. I jumped up to help, but he assured me he could manage and slid the tray neatly onto the table. He'd obviously done that before.

'Now, would you care to be mother?' I quelled my first oh-my-God nervous reaction and set about the business of fumbling with the milk jug, tea strainer and pot of Earl Grey. I felt like I had stumbled into a bygone era. Through the looking glass again, maybe.

The scones were perfect and I told him so – light, fluffy and fruity. 'Yes, as well as all her cleaning duties Sharon is a wiz at baking. It always used to be Bernard who had a light hand with cakes and desserts while my forte was the main course. My roast beef and Yorkshires were legendary.' He fell silent for a minute and I waited politely for him to continue. He pointed to the pictures on the mantlepiece. 'That's Bernard. Would you like to meet him?'

He invited me to step up with him to look at several photographs where Idris and another man smiled out at me, their heads inclined towards each other. They looked so similar with their neat haircuts, regular features and smooth skin they could have been brothers, but of course I knew they weren't. One picture was obviously from a few decades ago because both men were dark-haired then and well-muscled. They were proudly bare chested and wearing shorts, enjoying some sunny clime. 'Bernard, this is Rhian. She's come to live next door for a while. Isn't that nice?'

It could have been creepy, yet it wasn't. 'You both look so contented,' I said.

'Oh, we were, we were. Quite simply, he was the love of my life. It's been five years now since he passed away, and although I've got used to being on my own, I still miss him every day. We worked together as well, you see. Our little bookshop belonged to both of us, although the publishing press was more my area.' All the flamboyance had fallen away from him. I muttered the conventional words about how sorry I was and asked how long they had been together.

'Oh, decades, decades. Man and boy, you could say. We met at university and dallied with each other for a few years, on and off. Then the bookshop idea came up and that cemented us together, so we stopped being so silly and became a real couple. Oh yes, we were well known in our circle. When we went to a party people would say, "Hurray, Idris and Bernard have arrived. Now the party can really start".'

By this time we were sitting down again. I was fascinated as he told me more about their lives together. Then out of the blue he said, 'Have you had a great love in your life, Rhian?'

I had just taken a big bite of scone with a good dollop of cream, so my full mouth was an excuse not to answer straightaway. 'I suppose so. That would be my husband. We were married for nearly twenty-five years and we have a daughter. I thought most of those years was pretty wonderful.'

'And what happened to your husband?'

'He left. To live with another woman. At the time it was totally unexpected and it knocked me sideways. But now when I look back, all the clues were there. I just didn't want to see them.' I took another determined mouthful of scone. I had to stop this. Now. The past, with all its anguish and destruction, was starting to seep out through the well-constructed fibres sealing that time off in its box.

61

What was I doing anyway, telling all this to someone I hardly knew?

'Oh Rhian, I'm sorry. Do you know, I said to myself that there was a sad tale waiting to unfold. You have the air of someone who has seen hard times and yet survived.' His whole demeanour oozed sympathy; it seemed that even his bow tie almost drooped.

'Yes, I've come through. Well, you have to, don't you? I worked hard at my career and built my life up again.' It wasn't often, if ever, that I had said that out loud to someone and the sentiment gained validation by my speaking it.

'And there have been lovers, I hope? You're too lovely to have been on your own all that time.'

I was learning not to run for cover when Idris expressed his forthright curiosity, but to take it in the interested and warm spirit that it was meant. And the flattery was hitting the right spot.

'Oh, I haven't been chaste, by any means. No-one turned out to be special, though. In fact, I don't think I really wanted that.' Again, as I put the thought into words, the truth of it solidified. What had Idris put into my tea to make me open up like this? 'Not long before I came here for this year out, I broke it off with my latest boyfriend.' I stopped there. The tawdry details weren't interesting enough to be worth airing.

'Do you have any suitors now?' His eyes were twinkling, eager for a juicy snippet.

He had used the old-fashioned word without a hint of irony, as if it occurred in his everyday conversation. Perhaps it did. It made me sound like a nineteenth-century swooning maiden who was taking her pick from a queue of eager swains, which was a not altogether displeasing picture. 'Sorry to disappoint you, but suitors are off the scene right now. I want some time for me, to concentrate on reading and writing. And to get the stress from years of working out of my bones.'

With that we left the subject of my putative love life and diverted to what I was reading, his bookshop and small publishing house, and somehow from there we got onto to the merits and gossip of The Harp. It was another hour and two more cups of tea before I said I had better be going. We both commented, rather formally as befitted the occasion, how pleasant the afternoon had been and that we would do it again, or something similar, before long.

I'd never had a friend like Idris before. Oh, there were a few gay people I had worked with, of course, but I hadn't been in the habit of becoming close to any work colleagues. I remembered some of my girl circle used to say that everyone should have at least one gay friend. If they were like Idris, I could see why. Talking to him was like being on a therapist's couch. As I walked down the drive I felt uncorked, released, because some light had been shone into my backstory.

The grass-cutting man was gone now, and the garden exhaled the scent of the fresh mowing. It would probably be the last of the season; autumn was already getting a hold, and there was a hint of coolness in the air. Far from being a gloomy thought, it made me picture tranquil evenings in Heddfan with the curtains closed and a glass of red by my side.

Liminal

The windows give you back that wishful gaze.
Too painterly, the cottage of your dreams!
Step through the canvas, end the mirror-phase.

What if the past life imaged in its glaze
Were too close-tied to workaday regimes?
The windows give you back that wishful gaze.

'Get real' might be the homage custom pays
To some old stack of life-assurance schemes.
Step through the canvas, end the mirror-phase!

Dream-painted cottages may yet amaze,
Once entered, with their sturdy joists and beams;
No window then gives back that wishful gaze.

See how child Alice goes her dream-world ways
Around to ask: how sort out 'is' from 'seems'?
Step through the canvas, end the mirror-phase!

Trust her fresh optic lest that old one craze
Your vision, dull the sunlight as it streams,
And windows give you back that wishful gaze.

Here, now: your habitation! Count the days
As, room by room, this dwelling-space redeems
The canvas stepwise, ends the mirror-phase,
Has window-scenes dispel that wishful gaze.

Chapter 8

To travel west from my house near Slough to Lewis Cross, where I was renting the cottage, you simply got on the M4 motorway and stayed there until its end, beyond Swansea. Then if you wanted to go further beyond, you picked up the A roads, past Carmarthen to Haverfordwest, then north to Fishguard and a few miles more. You couldn't say it was a difficult journey, but it was long and it was boring, at least the motorway part was. After all, you were going three-quarters of the way across the country, and nearly 200 miles of that was motorway, past mostly unremarkable scenery. I set the cruise control on my car and listened to the various musical offerings on Radio 3 as I dodged in and out to overtake lorries and vans. But it could have been worse; at least it wasn't raining, when the spray from the big vehicles made you feel like you were struggling through a cloud. I vowed that next time I went home – and that wouldn't be for a few weeks – I'd take the train.

One truly impressive landmark on this road trip is the Severn Bridge. Its tall columns lick the sky and when you are on it you feel as if you are actually flying over the River Severn Estuary. When you have landed on the other side the sign that welcomes you to Wales soon pops up. When I saw that sign two thoughts came into my head, neither of which was true: firstly, it can't be that far now that I'm in Wales, and secondly, I'm nearly home. In fact it was a good two and a half hours to Lewis Cross, and hadn't I just come from my home?

Lunch was definitely overdue, so I pulled off into the next Services, where the signage was in both English and Welsh. It wasn't too busy. Even though it was the end of the school half-term week, most people were travelling back from holidays at the Welsh beaches to mundane English towns, and they would probably have wanted to do a greater part of their journey before taking a break. That's what I reasoned anyway, as I sat down with my pre-packaged chicken and salad sandwich, the tomato and lettuce all squishy. Nevertheless, I was hungry, so it was welcome.

My phone pinged and I saw that it was Lisa. She had sent me more photos of their new house, or at least the place she fervently hoped would be their new home, provided the sale of her house went through without a hitch. All in all, my visits to Lisa and family this week had been successful. She hadn't been very curious about my life in Wales, I suppose because she was so wrapped up in her own upcoming move. I was partly miffed about this and partly relieved. I hadn't wanted to justify how I was living and what I was doing, yet I had wanted to show off a bit about what a good decision it had been to go on this retreat. There was certainly less tension between Simon and I than there used to be, and he had chatted quite naturally to me. No doubt this was helped by my gift to them of £1000 towards their house move.

As I moved on to my cake and coffee the faces of the boys swam into my mind. They had both been enthusiastic about their new house and delighted to show it to me from the outside. Lisa had come too and she was just as excited. The house was already empty, so we had been able to stare through the windows to see the bare walls, with darker patches where pictures had hung and indentations in the carpets showing that furniture had been there. Was it my destiny to gaze in through the windows of houses? We even lifted the letter box and took turns to peep in to see the hall and doorways opening off it. Joe pointed to the upper storey to show me which his bedroom was going to be. Mum had said that his curtains with the aeroplanes on them would be able to come to the new house. They were a bit big, but she would make them fit, he explained earnestly. Knowing Joe's insecurity around change, it seemed a minor triumph that he was so engaged.

Then there was the day I had taken the boys to the zoo. To my pleasure and surprise, Nathan had wanted to come with Joe and me. Maybe it was the choice Lisa had given him between sorting his stuff or going out with Granny. Either way, we all had a grand day. From monkeys to alpacas, we visited them all and ended up with lots of photos. I was pleased that Joe asked so many questions about the animals – even if I was a bit hazy about the answers or had to rely on Nathan and Google. By the end of the afternoon, I have to say I was exhausted, but contented.

Yes, the time spent with my family had definitely been a success. What was less clear to me was my feelings about the time that I had spent in my own house. I looked at my watch. It was time I hit the road again if I was to get ahead of the afternoon rush hour traffic. I would mull this over some more when I got home. To Heddfan, I mean.

***

It amazed me that Idris was as fit as he was. We could walk together down to the beach at Pwllgwaelod, along the linking pathway to the tiny hamlet of Cwm yr Eglwys, which divided craggy Dinas Head from the mainland, and then back home. Right adjacent to the beach in Cwm yr Eglwys there stood just one wall and a tower of the ruined church, the one that was the result of devastation from storms over the centuries. After we had taken in the spell of the sleepy bay and its guardian church tower, we would walk back the same way. We'd done this four or five times now. Idris was a bit slow coming up the hill from the coast, but then, it was very steep, so I wasn't exactly sprinting up it. His walking cane that he always carried seemed more for show than for actually aiding him. Before tackling the hill, we had taken to pausing for a cup of tea in the shoreside café-bar at Pwllgwaelod, which today was almost empty, probably because the weather had turned windy and was now sprinkled with a light drizzle. The tide was fully in and the robust waves tore at the shore. I remembered how pleasant it was to laze in this bay when the weather was fine, but today you definitely wanted to huddle up indoors with a steaming drink and let the day go about its business outside.

Idris was as curious as ever. 'I'm glad your trip to visit your home and family was a positive experience. That's good to hear.' He sat forward and put his elbows on the table, moving aside the little jar of flowers that was decorating it. 'Now, tell me everything. It's two grandsons you have, isn't it?'

I did as he asked and told him about my family. He was beside himself when I recounted how Simon and Lisa had fallen in love again, and said it was the most marvellously romantic thing he'd ever heard. When I showed him pictures of me and the boys taken at the zoo, he declared that Joe was a splendid little chap and Nathan was a handsome youth.

'And what about you, Idris? Do you have anyone you're close to now?'

'Anyone I'm close to? No, not anymore. Oh, I've several chums around here, and I keep in touch with some of my London set, but no-one that I would call special. I've told you; I've had my great love. I've been luckier than many.' He didn't seem in the least bit sorry for himself, and I told him how much I admired that. He shrugged it off deprecatingly. Another couple came in, shaking the light shower from their jackets as they took them off. 'Thought we were going to get away with it,' said the man to us, indicating the overcast sky. He was middle-aged and rotund, with a wife to match. Idris replied conventionally while I smiled and nodded. I wondered what they made of us as a couple; they surely didn't think we were husband and wife – did they? – and Idris didn't look quite old enough to be my father. I thought they were going to prolong the conversation, but in fact they soon ambled off to a table near the window. Idris reverted to my time away.

'You stayed at your own house; I take it? How did that feel after your few weeks here in Lewis Cross?'

I was startled. I didn't know if he was being perspicacious, or it was just a lucky strike. 'Funny you should say that. It felt rather weird being there.'

'Oh? How so?'

The house had smelled musty when I first opened the front door, of tight-shutness and still air. I had gone from room to room and threw open windows, checking each room for disturbance as I went

68

round. My bed was made, the covers pulled tight and the pillows plumped. The shower still had its irritating slow drip. The fridge-freezer stood empty with its doors yawning. It occurred to me for the first time, that whereas my front door was opaque and therefore the mound of accumulated post couldn't be seen from outside, the wide-open evacuated fridge told clearly that the house was untenanted, should anyone be interested. I adjusted the fridge doors so that they were just slightly ajar, enough to give them the fresh air they needed to prevent mould. That was better. I left the cold tap running to get rid of stale water in the pipe while I gathered the pile of letters and junk mail and put it on the table to sift through. I thought how marvellous it was that no post came to Heddfan.

'It's like this,' I said to Idris. 'My house in England doesn't feel the same now. I thought I could just pick up being the old Rhian when I was there and be this emerging new Rhian when I'm here. But it wasn't as straightforward as I had thought. I know I will have to visit now and again to keep in touch with my family, but I think that will be all. I won't be going back until the Christmas holidays, and then not for long.'

Idris held his hands up in horror. 'You can't say that word in October!' I looked puzzled. 'You can't say it until December or at least the start of Advent! I shall get a swear box and insist that you put a pound in every time you utter the C-word before then.'

We both laughed. The couple at the nearby table glanced over at us and paused momentarily from eating their slices of cake.

'Seriously, I know what you mean,' said Idris. Once you've been bitten by the West Wales bug, everywhere else seems... superfluous.'

'Even though there's not much in the way of nightlife or big shops hereabouts.' It was part question.

'My dear Rhian, I could introduce you to a few pubs that take a rather liberal view about closing time...'

***

Friendship: two sonnets

So nice, our talk of this and that, of my
Life-story (bits of it) and his, this man,
Say 'elderly', not 'old', but older than
Myself by - fifteen years? - not one to pry
Beyond safe bounds, so just the kind of guy
I get along with. That's how it began,
This friendship, as our thoughts and memories ran
On tracks now close, now distant, so we'd spy,
At times, a certain kinship . . . How it stills
My restless soul, that talk of his: discreet
Yet unmisgiving; never over-spills
The private beans, has no wish to compete
For any hard-luck prize, and so fulfils,
For now, a need that no grand pash could meet.

And yet . . . Why then the moment's doubt when they,
A second couple, came and occupied
A table near our own, then briefly eyed
Us up, the two of us in that café,
And I thought quickly, oddly: who's to say
How we appear to them, what we've supplied
By way of clues, so gently gratified
We were by easy chat that might convey
'Long married, still in love'. And that somehow
Disturbed me, set me thinking 'no, you've got
Us wrong, please look more closely and allow:
The age-gap rules it out'. But then, why not,
Observing us, think friendship may endow
Two neighbours' tales with some romantic plot?

A wet and dismal dusk was starting to descend as I pulled the car into the space alongside the cottage. I let myself in through the front door and was met with a gentle waft of warmth. Near the end of November, with winter breathing down your neck, you needed to take the chill off a place like Heddfan. I imagined it would soon get damp if left unheated. As it was, the central heating worked perfectly well, although the boiler clanked and complained a bit. Still, the bedroom, sitting room and kitchen were served adequately by radiators, although the bathroom was not. I could see that showers would be speedy affairs in winter. As soon as I got inside the cottage, I closed the heavy curtains both to conserve the precious heat and to shut out the stealthy evening. I had started the evening curtains ritual after my trip back from England a month ago, when I had been relieved and contented to be once more ensconced in my new world of wild coast and tight walls. And poetry.

Going for the easy option, I took an individual lasagne portion out of the fridge and put it in the microwave to heat up. Then I got out the salad and prepared it. That meant opening one of those mixed leaves bags you get from the supermarket and adding some cucumber, tomato, grated carrot and dressing. I eyed the bottle of red on the worktop and hesitated. I would find it oh-so-easy to fall into the habit of drinking with every meal. After all, the French purportedly got away with it. But I was still clinging to the healthy notion of having two days a week without alcohol. On the other hand, today was decorated with a few mini celebrations, in its own way. What the hell, I pulled a glass out of the cupboard and sloshed generously into it.

I sat down at the kitchen table, with its the wooden surface scarred from decades of slipped knives and hot pots and reviewed my day while I tucked into my dinner. The first good thing had happened this morning when there was a garbled message from Lisa which I managed to interpret as being that they were all set to take over their new property. Contracts had been exchanged and the removal men were coming in a couple of days. Meanwhile they were tripping over the boxes which were packed and stacked in the living room. I messaged back and wished them good luck with what was after all a new and momentous stage in the life they had chosen to share. It would all be fine. I felt more reassured about it since I had seen something of the family together at half-term and witnessed what appeared to be the genuine affection between them. But you could never really know the inside story of a relationship. Let go and trust them, I told myself. Anyway, the move was underway.

Another positive thing today was that I had been out with Barbara and a few of her friends this afternoon. We had made arrangements to go to Theatr Gwaun, the lovely little theatre/cinema in Fishguard, next week. Barbara and I had also firmed up on her invitation that we had been mooting for the last few weeks, namely that I should go to have dinner with her and her husband in their home. Of course, that meant I would have to reciprocate sometime.

I put my fork down and glanced nervously round my domain, which was certainly scaled down compared to what I had at my disposal back in my house. We'd be a bit squashed at the table and the oven was a bit temperamental, but I'd do something simple and make it work. After all Idris had been here for lunch and that was fine. Really, considering I had only been in Lewis Cross for eleven weeks, my social life was humming and that was number two thing to celebrate. But I wouldn't want any more commitments or I wouldn't have time for writing. And that was why I was here in this beautiful part of the world.

I poured myself another glass of wine – why not? – and let my mind turn to the best thing of all that had happened today. After a few tense days of administrative feet dragging, I had eventually been informed that the Rental Agreement of Heddfan for the next three months was officially confirmed. So I could look forward to burrowing in and settling down for the dark December, January and February days that lay ahead. I anticipated with joy peaceful evenings in front of the fire writing, reading, listening to music, watching a bit of TV. Then there would be stormy walks on various beaches, invincible in my waterproofs, and expeditions to places

72

such as Cwm Gwaun or Newport with Carningli standing guard over me. *Step through the canvas, end the mirror-phase.* Like Alice, I was deep into the rabbit hole. It was where I chose to be.

Chapter 9

People with a December birthday often have uncertainties around celebrating it, and I was no exception. On the one hand I had a perfect right to hog a whole day to concentrate on myself, but on the other hand with Christmas only just over a fortnight away it was usually easier to let my birthday get subsumed into the general festive build-up. I'd chosen to keep my birthday low key for years; even my sixtieth birthday last year passed by relatively unmarked. I had intended to have a joint belated birthday/early retirement do, but somehow that ended up not happening.

Mam, I'm scared that Father Christmas won't come to me if he knows that I've just had presents for my birthday, and he'll say, "Well, Rhian, I think you've got enough, don't you?" Mam said that was silly and that if I was a good girl I would still get my presents. So she made me a birthday party with jelly and blancmange and a cake with candles on it. And we all played pass the parcel after tea. And Father Christmas did come after all. I didn't want to look under the tree on Christmas morning in case there was nothing for me. But he did come, he did. And he had drunk the glass of whisky that Mam had left on the bottom of the stairs for him.

How old would I have been then? Perhaps seven? I mused over this while I was digging out some opaque tights to put on under my woollen dress. It was the only dress I had with me in the cottage, and it felt like the occasion required it, along with a bit of jewellery and some make-up. I was quite excited: it's not every day that you get lunch cooked for you, let alone a special birthday lunch. It had all started a couple of weeks ago when I had innocently let it slip to

Idris that my birthday was coming up.

'Oh, my dear, you must let me take you out to dinner! Not just a meal in The Harp like we've had before, but a proper restaurant with an a la carte menu, a tablecloth and not a chip in sight. It will be my pleasure. There's a couple of suitable places in Fishguard or Newport, or we could look further afield.'

I graciously accepted, as you do when someone offers to buy you a slap-up meal. I hadn't had one of those since before I came to Pembrokeshire. However, it didn't turn out to be that easy to arrange. My birthday fell on a Monday, when most restaurants were closed. If we had left it a few more days, it would be even more firmly in the festive season and Christmas parties would have taken over. Idris said it wasn't right to have the celebration before my actual birthday. Then he hit upon his brainwave: he would make us a special meal, like he used to, back in the day.

'I've got it all worked out,' he said, holding his hand up to forestall my polite demurral. 'It will be a pleasure to cook for you. And I have some menu ideas. All you have to do is turn up and be spoiled. We can open one of my special bottles of wine. It's just such an occasion as this I've been saving them for.'

What could I say? It did sound enticing. So here I was, getting myself into the smartest outfit I had available, which I'm sure that Idris would appreciate. Eventually we had decided on a lunch, because it would be nice to eat with the daylight streaming in rather than with the curtains closed against the dreary December darkness. Also Idris, ever the gentleman, was worried about me tottering drunkenly down his drive in the dark on the way back, if it was late in the evening.

The day had started well. Since securing my second three-month tranche of occupation in Heddfan, I had begun having my mail redirected, and so I had some birthday cards arrive, which I had duly put up on the mantelpiece. One had been from an old friend from university, who never forgot my birthday. It was lovely to have her regular card. We didn't see each other nowadays, but she was taking early retirement next year, so who could tell? The excuse of busy lives wouldn't be valid any longer. Of course I'd had a card from Lisa, Simon and the boys, and I expected she would phone me after work.

Come at midday, he had said, and we'll enjoy an aperitif before lunch. I was surprised therefore to see it was actually Sharon who answered the door, not Idris. I'd seen Sharon a couple of times before at Idris's house, because she came in three mornings a week to clean for him, and to do various other jobs as required. It seemed to be a very flexible arrangement. I had taken to Sharon. She was very far from your stereotypical cleaning lady, being in her mid-thirties I should say, with baseball boots, purple hair and a nose piercing. From the couple of conversations we'd had, she seemed sparky, quick witted and cheerful. When I asked Idris what she was doing employed as a cleaner, he told me she used to be a nurse but now, with a five and a six-year-old in school, she only wanted to work for a few hours per week. And she lived in Lewis Cross, so it was convenient for her.

'Happy birthday to you, Rhian!' she said as she swung the door wide. 'Here, let me take your coat.' Her voice had the Welsh lilt that was always music to my ears.

I thanked her and sniffed appreciatively at the savoury smell emanating from the kitchen. 'Mmm, Idris had obviously been busy.'

'He's been chopping and stirring much of the morning, would you believe. So I stayed on a while to help him.' She reached her own coat down from the hallstand. 'And to ice the cake for the birthday girl, of course.' She was twinkling with vicarious pleasure. Or was she one of those people who did indeed get their satisfaction from making and doing things for other people?

'I'm sure it's going to be delicious,' I said. 'I'm as excited as a child! And talking about children, how are yours? Are they looking forward to Christmas?'

Sharon was winding a gigantic woollen scarf around her neck. 'Oh, you wouldn't believe! We got the tree down from the attic on the weekend and decorated it, and that really set them off.'

We were chatting about how magical Christmas is for young children when Idris erupted from the kitchen and enveloped me in a birthday hug, with kisses on both cheeks, and effusive apologies for not having been there to greet me.

'I have a bottle of champagne on ice for us,' he said, still holding my hands. 'Sharon, my dear, why don't you join us for a glass? You've been a godsend this morning and you'd be most welcome to stay.'

I liked and admired the egalitarian manner that Idris had with Sharon, with no suggestion that she was 'below stairs'. He really was a nice chap. Sharon said she wouldn't stay because she had too much to do at home. She kissed us both goodbye and exhorted Idris to look after himself. It seemed that she exceeded her job as cleaner and concerned herself with his welfare too. He was lucky to have found her.

So it was just the two of us that settled down to champagne and nibbles. Then we went through to the dining room where the table was graced with immaculate linen and Portmeirion tableware. The first course, which was smoked salmon and a salad with crusty bread in a basket, was artfully arranged on our plates. The first bite is with the eye, Idris informed me when I complimented him on his presentation.

The main course was brought into the dining room in style, in a hostess trolley. I hadn't seen one of those in years. Idris trundled it in from the kitchen – it squeaked a bit – and slid open doors to get out the warmed plates and various dishes with a flourish.

'There you are! Bernard and I used to swear by this little lady,' he said, laying his hand affectionately on her dark panelled surface. 'Back in the day, when we lived in London, we did *so* much entertaining you wouldn't believe. We would just load all the cooking into Veronica and *voila* – Bernard would wheel her in with such panache, and all in one go we were ready with our offerings. No trooping backwards and forwards with messy trays.' Idris sighed, lost for a moment in his memories.

I had to ask. 'Veronica?' I sought to contain my guffaw in case Veronica was the name of a revered aunt now deceased, or something like that.

Idris paused, a tureen of potatoes in his hands halfway to the table. 'Do you know, I really can't remember now. Well, isn't that ridiculous!'

We both burst out laughing, our mirth no doubt encouraged by the bubbles of champagne bursting in our brains, and we only calmed down because Idris pointed out that the food would be getting cold.

Well, what can I say about the meal? I hadn't tasted anything that good in many of the upmarket restaurants I used to frequent. Idris's centrepiece was a rich and herby beef bourguignon, a retro dish that was a staple of the bistro era. I remembered it well. He explained to me that he had balanced its complexity with plain accompaniments, namely potatoes and various greens.

We ate, drank and chatted. I could unwind in Idris's company. Yes, he was eccentric, but he was knowledgeable about a lot of topics, especially art and literary matters. Also, he seemed genuinely interested in me and my life, so we shared the conversation equally. He was a welcome contrast to the people with whom I had spent most of my life, especially my working life. I even took his signature bow tie for granted now. In fact, I hadn't ever seen him without one. We had both relaxed considerably by the time we were half-way down our second bottle, a most excellent Pinot Noir which Idris informed me was the perfect partner for beef bourguignon, although he confided shamefacedly that he couldn't bring himself to use a good wine in the dish itself, and it was just plonk for cooking. I assured him that it tasted divine.

'How is your writing going, Rhian?' Idris was bringing the serving dishes out of Veronica again so we could indulge in seconds. The food had stayed warm, so Veronica was earning her keep.

'Oh, steady,' I said, putting my hand up to indicate that one ladleful was enough. I had to leave room for the birthday cake, after all.

He waited. I concentrated on my food. When it was clear that I wasn't going to say more, he said, 'Oh you're so secretive and I'm so curious! I've seen the early work of several poets during my

78

years in the book world and it's always fascinated me. Even when it's not good, it's interesting. Often the deserving ones go on to get published. So you see I would be a very appreciative, not to mention experienced, ear.'

I had drunk getting on for a bottle of wine by this time which explained the wavering of my normal reticence, which must have shown in my expression.

'Oh please, Rhian. I would be honoured to see your early work. Then in years to come I could say, *Of course, I knew her before she was famous. Oh…*' He breathed in sharply and clasped his hand over his mouth.

'What? What is it?'

He leaned in close and laid his hand on my wrist. 'It's not pornographic, is it?' he whispered. 'Although I have read some dirty verse in my time.'

I gasped. 'Certainly not! It's all perfectly proper.'

'Ooh, I'm not sure I believe you. You'll have to prove it.' Was he starting to slur his words, or was it me?

I gave up. 'Alright, tell you what. I'll write a poem specially. It's going to be about birthdays and it's been tickling at the back of my mind for a few days now. I'll read it aloud to you, and you can read it yourself too. How about that?'

***

The short December afternoon was starting to dim by the time we had eaten birthday cake and drunk coffee and were slumped in armchairs in front of the fire.

'Idris, I don't know how to thank you. That was one of the best meals I've had in a long time. It's been a real treat.'

He waved his hand. 'It's been a pleasure. As your company always is.'

We both gazed into the fire embers. Replete, that's how I was feeling. Replete and boozily ruminative. 'I imagine you must have excelled yourself when it came to Christmas lunch,' I said, entertaining myself with the picture of Veronica bearing a steaming golden turkey, her wheels complaining at the weight.

'Ah, Christmas dinner. What an event that would be. In London we'd be about a dozen round the table, what with Bernard's family and friends who'd come round.' Idris went on to regale me with descriptions of the puddings that Bernard would make weeks before, lovingly dousing them with brandy at intervals. Then there was the main course, complete with all the trimmings. That was mainly Idris's domain. Only it was not turkey they had, but goose, he told me, his eyes dreamy with nostalgia.

'Goose?'

'Oh yes. That's the real traditional Christmas meat, not turkey.'

It was then that it hit me. I don't know why I hadn't thought about it before. 'What will you be doing on Christmas day this year? Will you be with anyone?' I think I knew the answer before I asked.

'Me? Oh, I expect I'll have a nice bit of chicken. That's what I usually do nowadays. And there's TV and radio for entertainment.' His cheerful demeanour didn't waver for a second.

I felt mortified. 'Oh, that's such a shame. I should have realised... what a pity I've arranged to go back home and see my family for Christmas.' As I said the words, the thought crystallised. I said it out loud while it was still newborn. 'I'm not going to go. I'm going to change my mind and stay here. Would you like to have Christmas lunch together?'

Idris paused, he definitely paused. 'You can't possibly do that. Your family will be expecting you, and your grandsons will be excited to see you.'

'Excited about their presents, more like. I'll go to see them a bit later, after Christmas. I actually think Lisa and Simon could do without me this year, to give them time on their own in their new home. And I'd have to drive because the trains won't be running, and it's a long and tedious journey.' All the doubts and inertia about this upcoming trip that I had been trying to push to the back of my mind burst out in the moment. Now I felt I had a justifiable reason for not going.

We looked at each other with dawning excitement at the

80

prospect. 'I'll help you to prepare the sprouts, peel the spuds and everything. I'll be your sous-chef.'

'My dear, it's an extremely tempting thought but are you sure this is what you should do? Won't your family be terribly put out?'

I considered. 'Do you know, I think they might be quite relieved to be on their own. Lisa will be phoning me this evening, so I'll tell her then. It's my birthday, so she wouldn't be cross with me, would she?' Would she?

***

I didn't have a printer at Heddfan so I had to go to a library to print out my poems. I guessed Barbara would have a printer which she would let me use, but I could just imagine her eager inquisitiveness as she looked over my shoulder at the emerging words. I wasn't ready for that. As it was, I decided I might as well print all the poems I had written so far, and I watched with some incredulity as page after page of text spilled out of the machine. Seeing my output collected together like this, and on sheets of paper rather than in small chunks on a screen, I was surprised how much it amounted to. I felt quietly satisfied and vindicated in my decision to commit to this retreat. I gathered the pages up and flicked through them. It was the same as with maps: you could look on your computer or phone and see a portion, but sometimes you also needed to see the big picture.

I had a few of the poems in my bag the next time I went to Idris's house, a few days later. We sat in the living room in our now customary chairs, drawn up towards the fire, as suited a December day. There were Christmas cards and fairy lights on the mantlepiece and other places, and a handsome Christmas tree in the corner, heavy with shiny baubles. I wondered if Idris had considerately avoided putting up his decorations until after my birthday, like Mam used to do.

We had paper chains that went everso high up, right across the ceiling, and balloons and lots of tinsel. Mam had to stand on a chair to put the paper chains up. We only had a little tree, which sat on the telly, but we did have a fairy for the top. She was the most beautiful fairy ever and her dress was white and her wand was silver. Mam lifted me up so I could put her at the very very top of the tree. And we had this thing like a little toy shed and inside it had little people and some animals. There were shepherds and angels and kings and Mary and Joseph. But the best of all was the baby Jesus lying in the hay.

We trotted out small talk for a while, and I wondered if Idris had forgotten the arrangement for me to bring some poems along. Even though I was nervous, I had psyched myself up now and I would have felt deflated not to go ahead with the performance, if that's what it was.

'Did you talk to Lisa about your change of plans for Christmas? I'm concerned that I might have caused discord between you and your daughter.'

Aha. So that was on his mind. Not unreasonably, given that Christmas wasn't much more than a week away. Was there discord between Lisa and me? I wasn't sure. When I had told her that I had rather not come for Christmas, she didn't try to talk me out of it, like I had expected. In fact she didn't say much at all. She had queried who Idris was; I had told her before, but I didn't expect her to remember the friends I had mentioned. I had played up the lack of trains over Christmas, and my reluctance to drive there in the winter. The truth was partly that I didn't feel comfortable about spending all that time with Simon. We were still tiptoeing round each other. And, as I'd said to Idris, I really felt their first Christmas as a reconstituted family in a new home deserved to be spent without me there. The boys I could catch up with a few days later. Then, there was the fact that I really loved my life here.

I decided to give Idris the simple, only slightly expurgated, version. 'It's all fine. Lisa understood why I'd prefer to stay here, so we're all good.'

'Oh, my dear, that's excellent news! I shall start planning this afternoon and write a shopping list.' He glowed with excitement, just like a child. 'Now, I hope you've brought that new poem of yours that you've written. I've been looking forward to it.'

So he had remembered. I got two copies out of my bag, all fingers and thumbs, and passed one to him. 'I thought I would read it aloud while you follow it. Would that be OK?'

The first time. This would be the first time I had read one of my poems aloud in front of anyone, even myself. I started; I stumbled. I cleared my throat and carried on. This time the words took wings and the poem was launched.

A Birthday

The birthday thing: its date comes round, you think
'Why flag it up, why celebrate, why plan
Another party? Shall your mortal span
Be stretched one minute just because you link

Up once a year with friends you seldom meet,
Or family with problems of their own,
Or maybe kids you thought had really flown
The nest until past episodes repeat

Themselves, most often this time in a mode
Part-trite, part faintly comic. So you take
The big decision, 'No more parties, make
Last year's the last'. But it's hard to offload

That kind of stuff, the kind that used to fill
Some part of every day, and often went
To leave its moody mark on periods spent
In doing sundry routine things, or spill

Across when I'd just snatched a moment free
From such unwanted worries. What's the use,
I ask myself, in striving to produce
The poetry I know it's there in me

To write if that means closeting away
The stuff, birthdays included, that may gift
Me life-events to write about and lift
My verse to meet what challenges it may.

The words died away, leaving only their subtle echoes, and Idris said nothing. He appeared to be reading the piece again, his fingers tracing over the words. I licked my lips and waited.

He put the piece of paper down and still he didn't speak. Just as I was venturing to break the silence, he said, 'I had no idea.'

I didn't want to hurry him. 'This is quality work. Your rhymes flow through the poem and carry it forward. Myself, I prefer an a-b-b-a rhyme scheme in a quatrain than the more usual a-b-a-b. It knits the whole thing together more effectively.'

I was astounded. This meant far more to me than the usual ostentation with which Idris tended to express himself. And he had revealed a knowledge of the mechanics of poetry I didn't know he possessed.

'Shall there be more like this?'

I laughed shakily, feeling the tautness inside myself loosen. 'I took the liberty of bringing a few along that I can leave with you.'

He took the sheaf of papers that I proffered to him. I watched as he glanced through the pages. He looked up and smiled. 'My dear,' he said, 'You truly are a poet.'

***

It seemed that here in Pembrokeshire the winters were mild, but cloudy and damp. Still, we had passed the shortest day now, the solstice, so I could comfort myself with the thought of the dark days gradually lightening as we trod the slow journey into spring. I had made a sandwich for my lunch, and the used plate sat beside me in my sitting room while I sipped my juice and contemplated, deliciously, the next poem that was assuming shape inside me. Christmas was one obvious theme, since it was only two days away, and I had re-read some classic Christmas poems to prompt my ruminations. *Bath salts and inexpensive scent, and hideous tie so kindly meant...* This morning Idris and I had been to the supermarket and stocked up on goodies for Christmas day, with the expected wrangle at the till about who should pay. I left him to store away the provisions and to plan his culinary strategy, which

85

seemed to be an exhilarating pleasure for him.

The rapping on the front door was an alien sound, resounding along the passageway. Who could this be? It was only infrequently that I heard it. I stood up, reluctantly, and parked my thoughts. Through the frosted glass of the front door, I could see the head-and-shoulders outline of a person, probably a woman.

It was Lisa.

Chapter 10

Mam had a beloved brother, my Uncle Fred, who had emigrated to America. He visited us a few times over the years, and there was always an orgy of frenzied cleaning that went on in our house for weeks before the great day when he and my new aunty, an American lady called Jean, arrived. Aunty Jean was like the queen of heaven to a little girl like me. She swanned about our place like somebody from a magazine, wearing make-up, jewellery and nail polish – nail polish! After all her hard work cleaning the house Mam was exhausted and frazzled during their visit and hardly able to enjoy it.

Then one day, I must have been about twelve I think, there was a knock on the front door. Mam was busy in the kitchen, Dad was sitting in the chair reading his paper as usual, so I went. It was Aunty Jean, and Uncle Fred was parking the car. No notice, no nothing. She was just there.

'Well, hello there, Rhian. Gee, you've grown.'

'Mam!' I called over my shoulder, my eyes goggling at Aunty Jean's bright pink lipstick and the ribbon in her hair. 'Mam, come quick.'

Mam came bustling out of the kitchen, muttering and wiping her hands on her apron. Then she caught sight of who was on the doorstep, which now included a beaming Uncle Fred, and she just threw her hands up and screamed. She yelled to Dad, 'Fred and Jean are here!'

'Don't talk so bloody daft, woman,' said Dad.

***

'Hello, Mum. Well, you did say you'd chosen to go and stay in the back of beyond. I believe you now.' When I didn't move, Lisa said, 'Can I come in? It's getting chilly standing here.'

'Lisa! How on earth... the boys, are they alright?' I knew really that they must be because Lisa was grinning cheekily, but it was first thing that ran through my head, quickly followed by, *Oh no, she's left him.* But again her impish smile made that seem unlikely.

She pushed herself in through the door – no thanks to me, I seemed to be frozen to the spot – and launched into a hug. Lisa, warm, solid and real. It was just as well she was holding me up as we lurched around the hallway crazily. Lisa, my girl. I didn't know if my gurgling signified laughing or crying. But you can do both.

Lisa broke away. 'I must have a pee,' she said.

I directed her down the hall and she raced in. 'God, it's a bit chilly in here,' she called through the door she'd left open.

'You get used to it,' I called back. I went into the kitchen and drew water into the kettle, pulled out two mugs and got the coffee from the cupboard. It's just as well you can do these things on autopilot. My brain was scrambling to cope. Lisa. She didn't belong here, in this part of my life. She lived in a different compartment. Yet here she was.

Lisa came into the kitchen, rubbing her hands briskly. 'Well, at least it's warm in here. Are you going to show me round, then?' So I showed her the other two rooms while the kettle was boiling. If I'd known I was going to be having company, I would have tidied up. As it was, yesterday's knickers were lying on the floor, the bed was unmade and in the sitting room piles of papers and books glared at us insolently. Nevertheless, Lisa seemed impressed – I think – with the cottage's compactness and slouchy retro comfort. Ideal for one person, she said. She asked what Heddfan meant, pronouncing it like an English person would instead of '*Heth-van*', and nodded approvingly when I told her it meant 'peaceful place'.

We sipped our coffee at the kitchen table, having cleared a space for our cups and the packet of biscuits I'd rustled up. I looked at her over the rim of my mug. She had a bright silky scarf loosely knotted at the neck of her jumper, teamed with what looked like new, unripped, jeans from Marks and Spencer's and boots. Her fair hair looked soft, bouncy and well cut. There was a veneer about her; she had blossomed since I had visited at half-term. Her new circumstances seemed to be doing her good.

'Aren't you going to ask me why I'm here on the day before Christmas Eve?' The smile seemed to be etched into her features.

'I'm too gobsmacked, to be honest. I haven't taken it in yet. You might be an apparition.'

'Well, here's the thing. You said one of the reasons you didn't want to come home at Christmas was that you didn't fancy driving. So here I am, your very own chauffeuse at your service. I'll stay the night here, because it's too far to do it all in one day, then tomorrow we'll jump in the car and off we go.' She was as excited as a child. 'I've been planning this. I couldn't wait to see your face when I came and surprised you!'

I attempted to get my head round it all. 'You came... you came all this way just to collect me?'

'I couldn't leave you here on your own, could I? Simon was happy to look after the boys – in fact he loves that – so I just had to make sure I'd got all the prep done first.'

My daughter had taken time out and come all this way for me. 'But... I said on the phone, I've made arrangements to have Christmas lunch with my friend next door. I hate to leave him in the lurch at the last minute.'

'I know it's a shame, but he'll understand, won't he? Phone him and tell him about the Christmas elf who turned up on your doorstep.'

That was why half an hour later I was dialling Idris's number. I stumblingly told him what had happened and apologised profusely, saying how awful I felt to let him down. He was totally magnanimous, as I might have predicted. 'My dear, of course you must go with your daughter. I will put the bird in the freezer and we'll have it at a later date. Don't you worry about me.' Then he insisted that Lisa and I called in for an aperitif on the way to The Harp, which I'd booked for our dinner. My daughter had taken time out and come all this way for me.

I knew Lisa felt awkward about meeting Idris, but she agreed it was the least we could do. She had fallen silent as we crunched down the gravel of his drive in the moonlight. 'Wow,' she said as we stood on the doorstep waiting for the answer to our knock. 'I didn't imagine anything like this. I thought it would be a little cottage like yours.'

The hall light flooded out as Idris flung open the door, punctuating the dark.

'Ladies, welcome! Do come in.'

I introduced Lisa. 'Ah, you couldn't be anyone else but Rhian's daughter.' His eyes swept over her appraisingly as he carried her hand to his lips and kissed it briefly before returning it gently to her side. Only Idris could do these things without appearing pretentious. I have to confess it amused me to see Lisa struggling to regain her aplomb.

He settled us in his living room and brought in a bottle of dry sherry and a dish of crackers. I didn't suppose that was Lisa's usual drink but she quickly adapted to the whole situation and fielded Idris's various questions – how was her journey, what did she think of Heddfan, would she go to look at the beach before we set off tomorrow, etc. I sat back and sipped, observing the interchange with amused interest and seeing how Lisa had relaxed by the time our glasses were refilled. She even haltingly apologised for taking me away over Christmas, but Idris wouldn't hear of it.

'I can see why you like him,' said Lisa as we hit the lane for The Harp. 'He's really sweet. I had wondered who this mystery man was that my mum had got friendly with.'

'Did you? I hadn't said that much about him.'

'That's precisely why I was curious.'

If Lisa thought we were going to have a quiet, anonymous meal in the pub, then she didn't know the typical folk of West Wales. By now I was practically a local, and so Brian who was behind the bar and a few regulars said hello and launched into conversation, with obvious intent to find out who the pretty blonde woman was. I felt proud of my Lisa as she politely dealt with the unabashed nosiness.

We were let off further interrogation when the meals arrived, and we fell into our usual safe space of talking about the boys. But this evening was different. The well-trodden grooves of irksomeness and prickles that usually lurked just below the surface of our conversations were less in evidence than usual. My daughter had taken time out and come all this way for me.

We strolled home in light drizzle, the torches on our phones guiding us. I say home, because it had become that to me while I was there. It was gratifying that Lisa hadn't turned her nose up at Heddfan, which made me realise how closely identified with it I felt. It was just as well she hadn't announced that she was coming for a visit, or there would have been hectic cleaning and pre-irritation about what she was going to think and say. I commented as much when we were flopped with our full stomachs in the sitting room, Lisa with her boots off and her legs curled under her.

'That's one reason I didn't tell you. And I didn't want you to make excuses for not coming with me. I've been worried about you, you know.'

'Worried? Why?' I was genuinely puzzled.

'Well, off you go into the wild west, to the back of beyond to live like a recluse, and your messages never seem... I don't know, they never seem authentic. It's like you're always trying to convince me you're OK.'

Why did Lisa and I move on separate paths, usually getting the wrong end of the stick? 'Are you reassured now that you're here?'

'Yes. Yes I am, actually.' She looked around the room and nodded thoughtfully. 'I can see why you're attracted to this little place.' She turned to look at me again. 'And this poetry that you've come to write. How's that going?'

Ah. What to say without wrecking this tentative link that we had established. 'It's going well, and I spend several hours most days working on it, but I'm not exposing it to the cold light of day very much just yet.'

She nodded. That seemed to satisfy her, and her interest seemed to slide away, thank goodness. She fiddled with a lock of hair as was her wont when she was thinking or anxious. Then she said, 'Mum, did you know that Dad and Janice have split up? She moved out recently. I didn't know whether to tell you.'

Well, that was out of the blue. What response did she expect, or want? Perhaps she'd think I might have gloated that the woman he had left me for was now leaving him after – how many years was it? – sixteen years. But all I felt was a reluctance to be interested in something I had completely cut out of my life.

'It's totally knocked him sideways. And he hasn't been well lately. He was really down when I took the boys to see him the other week.'

Even though you try, you try your best to disassociate from the memories, the hurt still seeps in if you let it.

She persisted. 'And what's happening to Dad now has made me think about how it was for you when he moved out. I never properly knew, because I was away at university, and I was with Simon, and you didn't say very much. Was it awful, Mum?'

Did we have to do this now, after we'd had such a nice evening? But she deserved some sort of an answer. She had taken time out and come all this way for me.

'Honest answer? Yes, it was. It totally dislocated my life then. But looking back, we had grown apart and things weren't right. Although it was painful at the time, it was for the best.' I hoped that would satisfy her, and she wouldn't want to probe further into things I couldn't put into words, even to myself.

'I'm sorry I wasn't there to support you.'

'Oh, I'm glad you were away. You'd have got dragged into it and that wouldn't have been fair.' I sought to repress the uncomfortable thoughts that were nudging, but actually there would never be a better time than this to say what was in my head, so I plunged in. 'Also, I'm sorry that when you and Simon came to live with me, I wasn't more supportive and well, nicer. It was enough just to cope with my own life back then and I didn't have much left over to give.'

Lisa reached over and put her hand on my arm. 'Oh Mum, it must have been difficult. I wish I'd understood more. But do you know what? Simon would have left anyway.'

Lisa's hand was warm. I decided to make another big effort.

92

'It's sad that Janice has left your Dad. We never know what's between a couple, do we?' Then I deliberately turned the conversation. 'Anyway, what about you and Simon? You seem much happier. It is really going as well as it seems?'

Her face lit up. 'It's like a miracle.' She then went on to tell me how idyllic their little family love nest was. I listened, made the appropriate noises and kept my maternal doubts to myself.

'But hey, since we're talking personally, what about you? Any romantic interest on the horizon?'

I think she would have been amazed if I'd said yes. So would I. 'Not at present. Now, it's time for me. But I don't necessarily rule it out forever. Watch this space.' Lisa had delved into the neck of her jumper and pulled out a necklace, which she was fingering. I could see the rich glint of gold. 'That's a lovely piece of jewellery,' I said. 'Can I see?' She had taken the hint that I didn't want to pursue the conversation and showed me the locket that Simon had bought her recently, with a picture of Nathan and Joe in each side. You had to admire how Simon treated Joe as if he were his own son. Not many men would do that.

Lisa yawned. 'It's been a long day, so I'd like to turn in soon if that's OK. I've brought my sleeping bag, and the sofa looks comfy enough. Or I can sleep on the floor, because I also threw an airbed into the car as well.'

I said I wouldn't dream of letting her sleep on the floor. She was a guest. I would take the living room. We wrangled, then eventually ended up in the double bed together.

We settled down like a pair of silly schoolgirls, fidgeting and giggling. I turned the bedside light off.

'OK, let's get some ground rules sorted for this bed-sharing business,' I said into the darkness. 'No snoring. No farting. And definitely, definitely…'

'Definitely what?'

'Definitely no cwtching up.'

'What on earth does that mean?'

'It's Welsh for a cuddle. I'm not Simon, remember.'

Lisa kicked me on the ankle.

Thank goodness the heating was turned up on the train back from Reading to Cardiff. That's what I needed after I'd just spent a day and a night back in my house. The cold had breathed at me as soon as I opened the front door; not just cold but that musty, still silence you associate with an unlived-in house. I had both flung the windows open to get the air circulating and slapped the heating on full. I inspected the place carefully, as I was obliged to do, of course, and was relieved to find that all was well. But I felt disorientated; my relationship to this place as home was slipping. No doubt it would come back when I came to live here again. I didn't want to think of that at present. That was next year. I went to the local shop to buy burgers and ice cream because I was having Nathan and Joe for lunch, while their parents did some DIY. Or just recovered gently from Christmas, perhaps.

I had to say it had been a great couple of days over Christmas. Lisa and I had had a leisurely trip to their house, chatting about inconsequential things, with both the weather and the traffic not too bad. Joe wanted to show me his bedroom straightaway, and he confided to me that his toys liked living there. Lisa had already warned me that he still believed in Father Christmas, so I knew I must tread carefully with what I said. Actually, it was a joy to go with the flow and embrace the festive rigmarole. Later when I snuggled down on the bed settee in their guest room which, unsurprisingly, was still chock-a-block with boxes, I eagerly anticipated the scene on Christmas morning. Some of Joe's excitement had rubbed off on me.

'Any drinks or snacks for you?' said a nasal voice from behind me. The refreshments trolley. I bought a coffee and a Kit-Kat and the trolley continued its slow progression. The coffee wasn't the best, but it was hot and welcome. I took my woolly hat off and undid my coat. At last some heat seeped into my bones and I let myself sink into the journey.

Christmas morning had been quite magical, with gifts and general mayhem. A morning of presents and jollity had been followed by a gargantuan lunch, clearing up, a few games and a film. A standard formula, no doubt adhered to by many families up

94

and down the land. It was good to see how Lisa and Simon interacted together, and how relaxed they were. I felt drawn into their family circle; I felt welcomed. Simon made a point of quizzing me about how I was getting on in my retreat, as he persisted in calling it. I had rather taken to the notion of being a poet on retreat. Lisa contributed that my cottage was really sweet and that I'd made friends with a dotty old gay guy who was generous with the sherry bottle. I shyly revealed in response to Simon's questions that I had now produced quite a lot of poems and my technique and confidence were improving. Lisa and I set about clearing the lunch debris and trying to get Nathan to help her. She didn't get involved in the conversation about poetry. At one time I would have let that annoy me.

I sat back and watched the skeletal trees glide past the train window, as we smoothly ate up the miles across the belly of England. No mighty Severn Bridge to cross when you took the train. Instead, it was an underworld transition from England to Wales via the Severn Tunnel. There was a slow descent into echoing darkness then you eventually popped out into the light again once you had crossed the divide. I was in Wales again.

It had been nice having both boys for lunch at my house yesterday, with a walk to the park tacked on afterwards. I think Nathan was glad to get out of his house after a few days cooped up with the parents and the little brother. After lunch he had said to me, looking down at his fingernails, 'You know this poetry stuff you've been writing?' I blinked. It was enough that he had noted what had been said, let alone that he was interested in it.

'For English we've got an assignment to do over the Christmas holidays. We've got to, like, get a poem written by a modern poet, somebody who's not dead, and submit it. We get marked for it.'

'Oh. I see. So you'd like me to recommend a suitable poet and poem?'

He shook his head, still very interested in his hands. 'Couldn't I have one of your poems? You're a poet now, aren't you?'

I was unbelievably gratified. OK, so Nathan might not give it more than a cursory read before he dismissed it as crap, but his teacher would probably read it. Was having a grandmother who was a poet something that was cool, or not? Anyway, I am a poet, recognised as such.

The little train wasn't there when we arrived in Swansea. Oh no! But it wasn't many minutes before it crept unassumingly onto the adjacent platform. I climbed eagerly aboard, bound for stations beyond Swansea and then, finally, further beyond.

Chapter 11

Dive deeper holding breath coming up for air seaweed bobbing on the waves cold I can see the beach but it's a long long way away swim swim towards the shore but wearing long coat flapping man waving to me man in a boat no car headlights on splashing through puddles was it rain spattering on the window the curtains blocked it out couldn't tell they are beige with big flowers on daisies I think it makes it dark in here even though it's not evening yet on the Coast Path the sea was spread out below me on one side and grassy banks on the other no flowers no daisies I was pushing a pram it was hard it was uphill I stumbled I held onto the pram but now it was a wheelchair John in it he turned round and smiled at me he had no teeth am I awake I can hear the sea washing washing or is it the rain am I awake I need a pee.

I lurched along the corridor to the bathroom, my head woozy and aching. I was cold, I was shivering. There was the sodden garden with dejected wet grass and hedges in the hardly light day. *Dive deeper, then delirium has free rein...* A hot water bottle, that was the thing, and a cup of hot coffee. I swayed while the kettle heated up and I concentrated to avoid scalding my fingers while I filled the bottle over the sink. Ahh! I clutched it against me and gulped its warmth while I crawled back to bed and burrowed under the covers. I sat up to drink my coffee and winced as the liquid passed through my sandpaper throat. Was it time for more paracetamol? I had no idea. I cwtched up to my hot water bottle and drew what comfort I could. I wished I was at home. I wished I could leave this nasty bug here and go home and be all better. My eyes drooped shut.

But I didn't want to sleep again. I had been sleeping or dozing on and off all day, and my dreams and half-dreams disconcerted me. Instead, I gazed hazily at the branched cracks running across the ceiling. That part to the left of the lightbulb... what did it remind me of? I know, it was like a witch's head. Yes, there was her chin, her ugly nose, her pointy hat. I turned over in bed so I didn't have to look. I supposed I could have read a book, but I couldn't summon up the energy. Instead, I lay and let the fragments of poetry that were bubbling up swish and swirl inside my head. *Dive deeper, then delirium has free rein...* I couldn't capture them in crafted, formulated lines, but perhaps that didn't matter for now. I just let them dance and clung on to their music.

Delirium

Come up for air and things start making sense;
Dive deeper, then delirium has free rein
And nonsense rules at poetry's expense.
Come up for air and things start making sense.
Deep down their meanings merge, collapse, condense
Till thinking creaks and cracks under the strain.
Come up for air and things start making sense;
Dive deeper, then delirium has free rein.

Secondary-process thought gives some defence;
Let primary process rip and what's the gain?
Just garbled dreams and meanings in suspense.
Secondary-process thought gives some defence
Against that sense-confounding chaos; hence
Sir Ego's faltering steps in id's domain.
Secondary-process thought gives some defence;
Let primary process rip and what's the gain?

A brief immersion gives some recompense;
Too deep, and visions craze the addled brain,
Yield Kubla Khans more vivid, more intense.
A brief immersion gives some recompense
Yet, though its gifts to poets seem immense,
Still poems move on a quite different plane.
A brief immersion gives some recompense;
Too deep, and visions craze the addled brain.

A Limerick

She said to herself 'That's mysterious;
My thoughts seem to me quite delirious.
If you've simply no choice
But to write like James Joyce
Then things have got pretty damn serious'.

Just to have had a shower and put some clothes on was progress, but it had worn me out. Although, I could cope with committing a few lines of poetry to my word processor. In fact, I had been eager to get some semblance of order to the words that had jingle-jangled in my head. This was, after all, the epitome of what I'd come to my solitary retreat for, this free flow of ideas and words that crystallised into poetry, my own poetry. For the latest poem I had used a repeated-line form (a *triolet*, which only uses two rhymes) that seemed to suit my half-dreaming state. Plus an impish limerick, just for fun. But it was a pity I had to get this horrible illness in order to achieve this super-creative state. I would have preferred it to be induced by drugs or alcohol rather than delirium. Still, today I was less feverish and my head and throat hurt less, but I was incredibly debilitated. And somewhat depressed and confused, to be honest. For the first time since I had been at Heddfan I felt isolated and a bit lonely. If I'd been at home – *home?* – my neighbour would have got shopping, Lisa would have enquired after me and even visited, work colleagues would have been solicitous. As it was, I had texted Idris to say I wasn't very well and played it down. He hadn't replied, but then, he wasn't a very good communicator with his mobile phone. I hadn't told Lisa so as not to worry her.

The rap on the door was sharp, followed by the sound of the letterbox being thrust open and a woman's voice calling 'Hello? Anyone there?' As I fumbled to disentangle myself from my laptop power lead, a mad thought leapt into my head that this was Lisa, magically appearing just when I needed her. But of course that was silly wishful thinking.

I goggled at the smiling purple-haired woman on my doorstep, taking a few seconds to realise who it was. I licked my lips and said 'Sharon'. My voice, which I hadn't heard for a few days, sounded croaky and frail.

'Idris said you were poorly, so I thought I'd pop round and see if you needed anything. And I've bought you some soup.' She patted her shoulder bag. 'I must say you don't look too good.'

She bustled ahead of me into the kitchen and I flopped down onto a chair at the table. Having ascertained that I'd like the soup straightaway she put the container into the microwave to heat up, then drew a chair up to the table opposite me. 'Now then,' she said, her nurse's eyes assessing me. 'Tell me all about it.'

Do you know, I could have cried. Here was a competent and caring person in my kitchen making me soup and letting me offload to her. I wasn't alone. She asked me what symptoms I'd had for the last four or five days, so I told her about the feverishness, aching, sore throat and general wretchedness.

She nodded her head 'Flu,' she said. 'That's nasty. But it sounds like you're over the worst.' The microwave pinged and she got up to give the soup a good stir. When she opened the door the most wonderful savoury aroma wafted out and I realised I was hungry. 'That's a good sign,' said Sharon when I told her. She searched around until she'd found a bowl and a plate for the crusty bread that she'd also brought with her. It nearly burned my mouth I was so eager to get the yummy nourishment inside me. It was chicken and vegetable, and I can honestly say that it was the best soup I'd ever tasted, and I told her so between mouthfuls and dipping my bread in the liquor.

Sharon beamed. 'I boil up the chicken carcass to make stock, then I pull all the meat off with my fingers and throw away the bones, add onions and garlic, ginger, cumin and whatever vegetables I've got lying around. I'm so glad you like it. That'll build you up.'

101

'It was just what I needed. I haven't been this ill for decades.' I kept some bread to clean round my dish so that I got every precious drop of soup. 'You're an angel, Sharon.'

'Well, Idris was a bit concerned. I said it wasn't a good idea for him to come round in case you were infectious.' She scrutinised me. 'You look a little bit perkier now, but it's probably going to be a couple of weeks before you feel completely well. Flu's a bugger.'

She said it with such reassuring authority. I feebly tried for lightness. 'I'm not going to die, then.'

Sharon smiled and shook her head, making her big earrings bob around. 'Not this time. Look, I can get you some things from the shop and drop them off tomorrow. Some fruit would be good.' She jumped up and poked around in my fridge, muttering as she did so. You'd think I would have resented this overstepping of personal boundaries, but I didn't. It was just such a relief that someone had taken charge. Neither did I mind when she said she'd just pop and make my bed, and asked did I want the sheets changed.

My phone pinged and a quick glance showed that it was a text from Barbara. 'That was my friend,' I explained to Sharon. 'She and her husband are away for a winter holiday in Tenerife. They're having lovely weather, apparently.'

'Ah, that's good to hear.' I didn't know if this approval referred to winter holidays or that I had at least one friend apart from Idris. Other people I had got to know since I had been here, pretty much limited to friends of Barbara's and people I had met in the pub, were not in the category of those who would administer succour to you when you were ill.

Sharon pulled out her phone and wrote a short shopping list on it. I marvelled that young people hardly ever resort to pen and paper, whereas I still made notes. Proper scribbles. She refused my offer to give her cash and said we'd sort it out when she knew exactly how much it all came to.

'Sharon, I can't tell you how grateful I am that you came round.' She waved away my thanks and stowed her soup container in her shoulder bag. Then she was gone, taking her breezy efficiency with her. But she would be back tomorrow. And I would be a little bit better.

I had the measles and I was all spotty. The spots were all over my body. Mam put some stuff on me to stop me scratching but it was hard because the spots were so itchy. Then the spots started dropping off me into the bed. Mam called them scabs. But instead of getting better I got really poorly and the doctor had to come. I had scary dreams but they weren't really dreams because I was awake. 'Now then Rhian, let's have a little listen to your chest, shall we?' said the doctor. Then he talked to Mam but I couldn't hear what they said and Mam had her worried face on. Then the doctor went away and Mam said I had something with a long name because I'd had the measles. I can remember what the long name was because I kept saying it and rolling it round and round in my mouth like a sweet. It was pneumonia.

***

As I turned off the main road in Lewis Cross I saw Sharon's car going the opposite way. I waved, but I don't think she saw me. Seeing her reminded of that time back in January, when she had ministered to me so kindly in my hour of need. She had been right, it had taken the rest of January until I felt completely myself again. I also remembered that back then, when I was feeling that all my strength had seeped out of me, I had vowed that when I got better, I would be grateful for my health and strength on a daily basis, and value it fully. That had been my intention, but the truth is you get on with the routine of your life once more and you forget.

It especially slips your mind if you step out of your routine, as I just had. Lisa had asked me if it would be any trouble to come and look after the boys for the second part of the half-term holiday. She and Simon hoped to go away for a romantic break and a belated celebration of Valentine's Day. No, of course it was no trouble; I would have been going to see the family around then anyway. It had turned out to be fun to spend some dedicated time with the boys, and to get over and done with the chore of checking that my poor abandoned house was faring OK over the winter.

103

Heddfan welcomed me back with its own now familiar smell and sprawl. Day by day this place, with its serenity and seclusion, continued to nurture me, away from the intruding world. The worst of the winter was now over, and March beckoned with its daffodils, primroses and quietly fattening buds. In fact, on March 1st, the day of St. David, patron saint of Wales, I would have been living in this peaceful place for six months. Six months! Where had it gone? But I had plenty to show for it – reading, studying and a ton of poems written. The thought I kept pushing to the back of my mind was that I was half-way through my sojourn, and from now on I would be sneakily counting the weeks I had left, no matter how I determined to 'live in the present moment', like wise people counselled us to do.

I had just received confirmation that payment for my next three months of tenancy, the spring months, had been received. My soul was cartwheeling with joy as I contemplated this. With spring on the launch pad, it was the season to begin planning some long walks on the Coast Path. It was an enticing prospect, and I was entertaining myself with my maps spread on the table and a notebook at the ready. I worked out by diligent study of the maps that the entire Coast Path would divide up into about twenty-five day walks. This was bearing in mind that I had to walk back as well, either by the same route or there was usually the option of navigating along lanes and tracks. I savoured the prospect of visiting these gems that I had discovered last year. There were intimate harbours like Porthgain, with its throng of small boats, secret bays only reached on foot, like Porthsychan, where if you kept your eyes peeled, you'd see a seal's head silently emerge from the sea, and parts of the coast in south Pembrokeshire where the red of sandstone took over the terrain.

So, bring it on! As spring got a hold the Coast Path would become less muddy, the weather improve and the hours of daylight lengthen. And the beauty was that I could pick and choose the days that I spent walking. If it was a poor forecast, I would stick to indoor activities instead and wait for fair weather. Also, I didn't have to do the walks in any particular order so I could let the microclimate be my guide, selecting from the more docile south near Tenby and Milford Haven up to the rugged parts in my own area near Lewis Cross, according to the weather forecast. I sat back and surveyed my crumpled maps and scribbled notes of routes and estimated times. It was intoxicating, all this dramatic coastline just waiting for me to stride over it again. I would even swim in the sea when summer put in an appearance.

I needed someone to share my overflowing ebullience with, and Idris was the obvious choice. I had phoned him yesterday when I got home from Lisa's but had missed him. He might have been in The Harp. I had also texted him, but of course he was notoriously poor at responding. I decided to descend on him and surprise him. Now was as good a time as any, so I abandoned the debris on the table, flung on my coat and trotted off.

The wind was quite cold but it was a dry day. Not bad for late February, I thought as I swung into the entrance to Idris's garden. The branches of the trees which flanked the drive waved like emaciated limbs, and snowdrops were sprinkled in the grass. What's this, there was a car on the drive. It was a gleaming 4x4. Not the sort of car I would own, but then, all I really cared about was a wheel on each corner and as much reliability as possible. I paused. Perhaps if Idris had a visitor I should go home and phone him later. But I was here now, and I wanted at least to say hello to Idris and let him know that I was back again. What I really sought was for him to be a mirror for my delight – another three months' rental in the bag, and all these walking adventures in prospect. And I admit I was curious about the visitor.

My smile was ready to greet Idris when he opened the door. Only it wasn't Idris, it was a slim man, perhaps a couple of years younger than me, wearing smart trousers and sweater. I deflated under his enquiring scrutiny. 'Oh,' I said. 'Is Idris there?'

'No, I'm afraid he's not.' His voice was educated, firm, English.

I was flummoxed by the appearance of this smooth stranger inside Idris's doorway. A lover, perhaps? But then why wasn't Idris there? It didn't make much sense.

'Excuse me,' I said, in my best polite voice. 'But who are you, exactly?'

'I'm Idris's son,' he said.

Other Lives: a terzanelle

Strange how the lives of others reel you in.
Almost it seems you live them as your own.
Strange how the lives of others reel you in.

A risky thing: don't want your cover blown!
You've changed lives once, why do it yet again?
Almost it seems you live them as your own.

It's mirror neurons, so the books explain:
They fire, then lives begin to intertwine.
You've changed lives once, why do it yet again?

And yet, you think, how sever his from mine?
'No man's an island', as the poet wrote.
They fire, then lives begin to intertwine.

The best you'll get's a life-line asymptote,
No new life bang on target, just as planned;
'No man's an island', as the poet wrote.

Chance has a hand in it, a hidden hand.
Lives swerve from every point of origin.
No new life bang on target, just as planned;
Strange how the lives of others reel you in.

It's through chance meetings those new lives begin:
No time at all, you're in the transit-zone.
It's through chance meetings those new lives begin.

You get on, find the friendship's quickly grown,
New neighbour, maybe, on his home terrain:
No time at all, you're in the transit-zone.

As in a terzanelle, your lives entrain;
They meet, cross paths, divert from line to line.
New neighbour, maybe, on his home terrain.

Few more encounters and you're out to dine;
Your old new life's a 'fresh start' got by rote.
They meet, cross paths, divert from line to line.

Then it's your old old life that feels remote
Till some plot-detour has you understand
Your new life's now a 'fresh start' got by rote.

Truth is, your whole life-story's one that's spanned
Each episode, each latest novel spin,
As some plot-detour had you understand
All those chance meetings where new lives begin.

Chapter 12

Normally I make a point of climbing stairs rather than using a lift if I can, so as not to waste any opportunity for a bit of exercise. But here the ramified corridors and turnings seemed to be a confusing labyrinth to me, cluttered with laboriously pushed wheelchairs and people hobbling doggedly with sticks. So, when I saw a signpost to 'All Wards' I latched onto it and hopped into the welcoming lift that promised to take me where I wanted to go. I was vaguely aware of the silent couple next to me; she was sniffling quietly into a handkerchief; he had his arm around her. You don't generally make eye contact with people in a hospital lift, and accordingly I obeyed the etiquette and kept my eyes on the corner of the lift where a sweet wrapper lay discarded. The lift whimpered to a halt at the next level. A man with a bunch of flowers in one hand and a mobile phone in the other got in, and we continued our vertical journey. Hospitals weren't my favourite places, but I suppose most people would say that.

I found my way to the ward front desk and waited quietly while telephones were answered and a couple of admin people frowned into computer screens. A doctor went behind the desk and pointed out something on a clipboard to a nurse. This was followed by a short discussion and curt nods, which seemed to resolve it. You could tell she was a doctor by the stethoscope slung round her neck like a garland, rather than any suggestion of age or gravitas; in fact I could almost have taken her for a sixth-former. When did doctors get to look so young? Probably at the same time teachers and policemen did.

Having got directions, I headed into a side ward, which

accommodated six beds. Three were festooned with visitors in various levels of engagement with their visitee. Next to them was an old man hunched and alone in a chair beside his bed, staring vacantly across the room. One bed was screened off, and I could hear faint moaning and other, authoritative, voices. I didn't care to think about what was happening behind those curtains. Idris was at the far end, by the window. God, I nearly didn't recognise him. He too was sitting in the bedside chair, his garish pyjamas hanging loosely on him. There was a nasty bruise on his forehead and his hands hung palely off the arms of the chair. He seemed to be hooked up by a tube to a bottle on the floor which contained a yellowish fluid stained with blood. He had aged ten years.

'Hello, you,' I said, in my jovial visitor voice. 'What have you been doing?' He turned his bleary gaze and it came slowly to rest on me.

'Rhian! How lovely to see you.' His speech was slightly slurred and I realised that his slow responses were probably because of drugs. Strong painkillers, I imagined. I pulled up the visitors' chair close to him and took one of his hands, where it lay flaccid in mine.

'I'm so sorry to hear about your accident. You fell downstairs, I understand.'

I had to lean in close to pick up all his mumbled words. 'Don't... don't really remember what happened. I was lying at the bottom of the stairs with an agonising pain in my hip every time I tried to move. So I stopped trying to move.' I squeezed his hand and waited, relieved that his dry sense of humour was trying to surface. 'Must have blacked out because the next thing I knew the paramedics were there and Sharon... Sharon was ordering them about.' He was lucid, I noted, just slowed down by the medication, and his eyes were a bit unfocused.

'Thank goodness it was one of her days to come and clean, or you could have been lying there for ages.' I felt his fingers stir in mine. 'They've operated and given you a new hip, is that right?' He nodded his head slightly in assent. 'It's wonderful what they can do nowadays. And I'm amazed they've got you out of bed already.'

'No rest... no rest for the wicked.' His lips twitched towards a wobbly smile. 'You have to move about a bit as soon as you can.' His unheld hand was straying towards his water jug. I poured some water out for him and supervised as he lifted it to his lips. Who was this old man?

I enquired about the bruise on his head, but he didn't seem to know it was there and fingered it wonderingly. I asked him how long he would be in hospital, but he didn't know. My mind skipped ahead to when he would come home. It was fortunate that he had a downstairs toilet, and presumably arrangements would have to be made for him to sleep on the ground floor temporarily. We made the conventional conversation about the food in the hospital, and what the staff and his fellow patients were like. He didn't have any complaints, but then Idris wasn't the complaining type. He even asked me, in his slow whisper, how my visit to look after my grandchildren had gone – he'd actually remembered. But he didn't mention anything else.

I could see that he was getting tired now, and his eyelids wanted to close. I kissed his cheek and told him I would see him again tomorrow. I retraced my steps, past the desk which was still abuzz with industrious staff, down the corridor and into the lift. The discarded sweet wrapper was still there in its corner, and it shifted slightly on the draught as the lift doors closed. Oh Idris, you looked so poorly. I hope they look after you in here and that you heal quickly. And why didn't you tell me about your son?

All Wards

'All Wards': the first sign leaves you room for dread,
Hope, every shade between - Ward Ten, the one
You're visiting, signposted 'straight ahead',
Past scenes of life restored, drawn out, undone.
You count them off, each ward, now you've begun
This tour of stark vicissitudes, this tale
Of lives elsewhere - in hospital, in gaol.

Out-patients One to Three, the usual run
Of minor injuries, you think, and shed
A few misgivings, but the yarn you'd spun
Yourself of finding him sat up in bed
And chatting merrily gave rise instead
To queasy thoughts of where this lengthy trail
Might end if One-to-Ten defined the scale.

'Ward Six: Neurology', the next sign said,
Then 'Seven: Cardiology', and none
More worrying than Eight and Nine which fed
Your darkest premonitions with their un-
Revealing numerals, as if to shun
Your anxious gaze. Ward Ten: don't let them fail
You now, those nerves: how old he looks, how frail.

'Are you Sharon?' He had held the front door only half open.

'No, I'm Rhian. I'm from next door. Where's Idris?' I had craned my neck to try to see past this man and into the house, but he was pretty much blocking the view. He couldn't be some sort of intruder or con-man could he? But then, he'd mentioned Sharon. My heart was starting to pound as I grappled to weigh up the situation.

He sighed and let the front door swing open. 'You'd better come in,' he said. He had a featureless middle-class accent.

I hesitated. My fingers closed round the mobile phone in my pocket.

'I'm Tim.' He held out his hand. 'Idris has had a bit of an accident, I'm afraid.'

I hesitantly shook the proffered hand – a firm handshake – and stepped inside. 'Is he... is he alright?'

'It seems that he took a tumble downstairs. He bashed himself about somewhat and broke the neck of his femur. They carried out a hip replacement yesterday.'

I blinked at him, my mouth probably hanging open. This news, given so formally and coming after the doorstep disclosure, left me reeling. 'He is going to be OK, though?'

'The operation appears to have been a success and he is comfortable.' He looked at me appraisingly. 'Rhian, you've just had a big shock so–'

'Two big shocks,' I interrupted.

'Quite. So I think you should sit down for a while and have a cup of tea or coffee.'

I perched on the edge of the chair in the familiar room. I tried to concentrate on the reassuring kitchen sounds of the kettle boiling and the fridge door opening, but knowing it wasn't Idris making those familiar noises; it was this stranger. Idris was lying in a hospital bed somewhere. I felt lightheaded and dizzy so I sat back in my chair and breathed deeply.

He brought in two mugs of coffee and sat down. I didn't know Idris possessed mugs; he always used cups and saucers for me. I lowered my head over my drink and looked covertly at the well-turned-out stranger opposite me. The clock on the mantlepiece continued to drip its tick into the silence between us.

'It seems that his cleaning woman found him on the floor in the hall when she came for her regular work shift three days ago, and called the ambulance. When he was admitted, he must have given me as his next of kin and the hospital contacted me. I came as soon as I was able. It's fortunate that I was on leave anyway for a few days.'

'Can I visit him?'

'That would be very kind of you. I have to go home soon.'

'And as far as you know he's not in danger?'

'No. The operation was a success and now it's a matter of recovery and convalescence.' He paused and crossed his legs. How well polished his shoes were, I noticed. 'I'm a surgeon, you see, so this is entirely my country.' Yes, I did see. It fitted his demeanour, his conversation, his grand car outside

Idris lying in hospital. A man who claimed to be his son appearing. How do you get your head round something like that? I took another glug of coffee, a deep calming breath and decided to go for it. After all, he was going home tomorrow and then I would have missed my chance to question him.

'I've been friends with Idris for a few months now, and he's never mentioned you. And, forgive me, but you look a bit too old to be his son.' I could have added that Idris was gay, and he'd implied that he always had been.

'Ah.' He stared at the coffee table between us, where half a dozen books lay higgledy-piggledy across its surface. One was face down and open on the top of the pile. I supposed that was what Idris was currently reading, and perhaps I could take it to him in the hospital. 'I didn't know I was such a complete secret.' He continued to frown ruminatively, as if deciding how much to divulge. Then he said, 'Idris was eighteen when I was born. I can only vaguely remember him when I was very young. He left and my mother married again. I always considered that man to have been my father.'

I digested this as best I could. 'Did you and Idris keep in touch?'

114

'Rarely. We always knew where the other was, 'just in case', but 'just in case' never happened until now. Frankly I'm amazed that Idris knew my address and phone number, so he was able to provide my details at the hospital.'

I nodded. 'Are you staying here?'

'Oh no, I'm staying at a hotel. I'm here because Idris asked if I would get some things for him.' He wasn't looking at me but staring steadily at the mantlepiece. I followed his gaze, where it was resting on the picture of Idris and Bernard together.

***

It's amazing what a difference a day can make. Whereas Idris didn't look his normal vigorous self, he was certainly better than he had been the previous day. Today he was more alert; he spotted me coming into the ward and his face lit up.

'Rhian, my dear! I am so pleased to see you.' I noticed that today his eyes were clearer and more focussed, and his hands less fumbling. I presented my gifts, which were chocolate biscuits and grapes. I had been lucky enough in my life not to have done much hospital visiting, but I did know you're always supposed to take grapes, even if only to have something to nibble while you chat to the patient. I had also taken in spare pyjamas, tissues and his book. He was very pleased by all this and didn't take much persuading to have a chocolate biscuit. On his bedside cupboard there was a big 'get well' card – which I hadn't thought of – signed by Sharon with lots of kisses.

It turned out that Idris didn't remember much about my visit the previous day. 'I can just about recall you being here, but not what we talked about. It's a bit like a dream.'

'You seem much more with it today,' I said, with relief. Seeing my friend change from someone who I thought of as not very senior to me to an old, ailing man had been upsetting. 'Are you in much pain?'

'No, they're keeping that all under control. And the staff are all sweeties. Here's one now.' He smiled at the young nurse who

115

approached him with her trolley. 'How are you doing today, Idris?' she said, her voice a mixture of brisk efficiency and kindliness.

'All the better for seeing you, my dear,' he replied while his blood pressure and other vital signs were being measured. I was pleased to see his customary jauntiness reappear and I let them enjoy a bit of banter while my thoughts returned to the message I had received from Tim this morning. I covertly pulled my phone out of my pocket and read it again.

Dear Rhian, on reflection, I might have been a little abrupt and guarded when I met you yesterday. It was quite an unprecedented situation, wasn't it? I understand that you and Idris have become friends over the past few months and that you are going to continue being so. Therefore you probably deserve rather more explanation and courtesy than I have hitherto given you. To that end I wonder if you would be free to be my guest for dinner this evening? I'm staying at the Red Lion in Newport, but I am happy to eat wherever you suggest. It is, after all, your territory. Regards, Tim.

The invitation had taken me by surprise, and it had left me with mixed feelings. For one thing, it had softened my view of Tim. He had clearly been thrown by recent events too and it was magnanimous of him to have admitted his standoffishness. After all, when he had been contacted by the hospital about Idris's accident, he had taken the trouble to come, which he didn't have to. And I admit I was curious about the whole unprecedented situation of this skeleton in Idris's cupboard, who turned out to be Tim, and I wasn't going to miss the opportunity of finding out more. Then there was the opportunity to go out for dinner. Indeed, what wasn't to like? So it hadn't taken me long to thank Tim for his invitation and to tell him that I would meet him at the Red Lion this evening.

Having said a cheery goodbye to Idris and included me in her smile, the nurse carried on her procession from bed to bed. Idris and I continued to pass the time with inane hospital talk, while I kept a watchful eye to see that he wasn't getting too tired. Even though he seemed to be doing very well it hadn't been long since

116

the hip replacement, plus the fall in the first place, and I didn't want to overtax him. I was so tempted to tell him that I was going to meet his son that evening, but I didn't. He probably thought that Sharon had told me about his fall, and I decided to leave it that way. For now.

Chapter 13

I'm glad that we were meeting at the Red Lion. It was only three miles up the road from me and it was a pub that rated highly on the recommended list. You wouldn't quite call it a gastropub (they don't go in for that sort of thing much round here) but nevertheless it had a Bar with welcoming touches like plenty of brass bric-a-brac and a menu that featured slightly adventurous meals yet still with a homemade feel. It was a notch above The Harp, and anyway, that was definitely out as a venue. I could just imagine eyebrows raising and tongues wagging if Tim and I met there.

He was already standing at the bar with a gin and tonic when I arrived. We shook hands and greeted each other pleasantly. I'm ready for this, I thought as we sat down. The other day I was wrongfooted because I was ambushed by the shock of it all. Now I'd had chance to absorb it, seen Idris a couple of times and been reassured that he was over the worst, I was up for the challenge of engaging with this man. I sat back and smiled, exuding relaxation. Bring it on.

I grabbed the conversational lead. 'I've been to visit Idris twice. I was amazed at how much better he was today, whereas yesterday he just wasn't with it. Today he talked quite normally, although he was getting tired by the time I left. He's moving round a bit, too.'

'Good. It's important that he should have started walking.' As Tim talked more about Idris's forthcoming rehabilitation, I noticed that the fingers of his left hand, long, slim surgeon's fingers, were drumming softly on the table. So he was nervous. Perhaps he was not as in control as he would have liked to convey. I also noticed that he wore a wedding ring.

118

'Do they have any idea why he fell? Was it a heart attack or something?'

'That has been thoroughly checked out and nothing of the sort was found. And I did look in his house and found a ruck in the carpet at the top of the stairs, so it was almost certainly a simple trip. He's lucky he didn't injure himself more. As it is, he'll probably be home in a few days.'

'A few days? Really? I thought it would be longer than that. How on earth is he going to manage at home?' As I said this I felt a guilty pang as my mind sped over the implications of a semi-helpless elderly man right next door. I was happy to visit, keep his spirits up and do a few chores, but nursing… that was outside my experience and my comfort zone.

As if reading my mind, or more likely my expression, Tim said, 'I'm going to arrange for a nurse to come in for the next couple of weeks, which should be enough.' He didn't say who was going to pay for this, and it wasn't my place to ask. 'After that he will probably be able to see to his own personal needs. Apparently, his cleaning lady found him at the bottom of the stairs, so she knows about the situation. I hope she'll continue to come.'

I nodded. 'I can get in touch with Sharon, and we'll sort out when she's to start coming again. She's a lovely person.' My mind flashed back to those dark January days when Sharon had been my lifeline.

We turned out attention to the menus. While Tim was considering his choice, I took the opportunity to appraise him. He was certainly smart and well groomed, with perfectly trimmed and combed greying hair, a smooth complexion and a classy designer sweater. And then it hit me. I was looking at Idris from years ago; it was something about the head shape and the curve of the eyebrows.

Tim looked up sharply and I wasn't quick enough to withdraw my scrutiny. Instead of looking away, he met my gaze and held it. I dropped my eyes first, aware that I'd been caught out. I decided to be honest. 'Excuse my rudeness, staring like that. But you see, it just struck me how much you resemble your father.'

He flinched, and I immediately regretted my remark. 'I'm sorry.

That was a bit insensitive.'

Perhaps it was fortuitous that the waiter stopped at our table then to take our order. By the time that conversation was done, including his recitation of the specials, the flashpoint moment had passed.

'So, Rhian,' said Tim. 'Tell me a bit about yourself.'

He had regained his poise. I regaled him with my story of how I had retired early and had a yen to spend some time, namely one year, living alone in this part of the world, since I had no ties, to explore both the beautiful coastline and my own ability to produce poetry. I was taken by surprise at myself, that I revealed my aspiration quite so readily. Did that mean I was growing into the role of poet?

'Ah, so you're not resident here. When does your tenancy end?'

Presumably he was thinking about how long I was going to live close to Idris. 'Well, I'm half-way through, so the end of August.'

'And do you return home then?'

Do I return home then... The ramifications of the question caught me unawares. I supposed I would be going back to my house. But I didn't want to think about that yet. I had survived wonderfully through the dark time of the year and now the best was to come; the gradual lengthening of the days, new leaves and wildflowers erupting in the spring, the exuberant bloom of summer. I felt the wild uncurling of my soul accompanying those thoughts. Meanwhile Tim had asked me a question. 'I had always intended that this sojourn, if you want to call it that, should be a year to encompass a complete cycle of seasons.'

Tim started to reply, agreeing with my reasoning, when the harsh signal of a message on his phone interrupted us. The couple at the next table glanced our way. 'I do apologise,' said Tim. 'I could have turned this damn thing off.' He scanned the phone briefly. 'It's from my son, but it's not urgent. You see, his wife is expecting her first baby in a month's time, so I like to keep communication channels open between us if possible.'

I digested this. So not only did Idris have grandchildren, but he was soon to become a great-grandfather. Oh Idris, do you know this? For the rest of the meal, we got onto each other's histories. By the end of it he knew about my family and career and I had learned that he was a consultant surgeon, his wife worked part time, they lived near Bristol and had two children, both married.

It was when we had retreated to the Bar that I took the plunge. 'Tim, would it be impertinent if I asked you to tell me a bit more about your relationship with Idris over the years? You see, he must know that I know, and he's bound to say something.'

A muscle moved in his cheek. 'Yes, I suppose that's reasonable. Well, here goes. A potted version.

'I don't remember Idris in my life when I was very small. I learned later that he had left my mother when I was just a few months old, and she met and married the man I call my father a year or so after that. I do remember this rather flamboyant character whom I called Uncle Idris used to come and visit about two or three times a year and bring me presents. As time went by I became curious about exactly who this Uncle Idris was, and one day my mother told me. I would have been about ten at the time.

'You can imagine the confusion this bombshell produced in a boy of that age. I just didn't understand. I completely rejected Idris and clung to the man I knew as my father. So there were no more visits from Uncle Idris. It was only a few years later, when I started to become aware of such things, that I worked out he was gay, even though he'd obviously had a relationship with my mother before he'd "come out". Of course, that was a much bigger deal back then than now. Once again, I confronted my mother and she confirmed it. It also became apparent how bitter she was about the whole thing. Apparently he had been trying his best to be "normal" and that was how come he had got my mother into trouble.

'When I went to university, I took it into my head to get in touch with him again. Perhaps I thought it gave me some kudos among my peers to have a dad who was gay. We met a couple of times, but it didn't really gel. He was part of the London gay scene and a rising star in the publishing and literary world, and I was a student studying medicine in the North of England. We didn't fit into each other's lives. And, as far as I was concerned, I already had a dad.'

121

There was about half a dozen men at the other end of the Bar standing in a group clutching their pints and talking, obviously locals. Every now and then a guffaw reached us, but not so loud that it disturbed our conversation.

'The relationship, if there ever was one, drifted into occasional contact mainly to tell news, such as when I qualified as a doctor. Then longer and longer times, years I mean, would go by between us acknowledging each other's existence. So there never really was any sort of bond, as such. He did inform me of his address when he retired to West Wales, and I assumed it was with his partner, who was never spoken of. I notified him when my mother died a few years ago. I thought he might show up at her funeral, but he didn't. I was rather glad.'

We were both silent for a moment after Tim's mechanical recital. As for me, I was just struggling to get my head round those revelations. The crowd at the end of the bar were now drinking shorts. Two of them were wriggling into their overcoats ready to head into the February night.

'Thank you for telling me all that,' I said at last. 'Presumably Idris had cited you as his next of kin, and that's why the hospital contacted you?' Tim agreed. 'But... I'm not sure...' I struggled to ask the question. Maybe it wasn't my place. But I went ahead anyway. 'Given that you say you didn't have a relationship with Idris, why did you take the trouble to come and visit him now?'

'Ah.' Tim leaned his head back against his chair and fixed his gaze beyond me. 'Several reasons, I suppose. One was that my wife said I should, and she's always right.' We exchanged a brief smile about this touch of humour. 'And it was a finite possibility he might die, so I felt I should be on hand. Then I was simply curious about this place he was living in.' He shrugged. 'So here I am. The ties of blood do count for something, it seems.'

'I hadn't really thought that he might actually die.'

'Well, he is nearly eighty and before I saw the state of the carpet at the top of the stairs, and the diagnosis was in, I thought it was entirely plausible that he might have had a heart attack.'

'*Nearly eighty?* I can't believe it!' Nor could I. He was – or had been – so sprightly, so vigorous. We had often walked together, him swinging his cane and striding along. I thought of him as older than me, but not old enough to be my father. He had never said his age; but then I had never asked.

The barman came bustling up to us to collect our empty glasses, a subtle signal that he would like to be closing the Bar, since it was now empty apart from us.

I thanked Tim for dinner and for being so frank in telling me his story. There was a lot more that I was curious about, such as some details about his wife and kids, but that wasn't really my business. 'Will you be keeping in touch with Idris now?' I said as I put my coat on and gathered up my bag and scarf.

Tim didn't answer straight away. 'I don't think so. I've seen that he is OK and I've arranged for care when he comes home.'

'Would you like me to keep you updated with how things are going?' I wasn't sure why I was persisting.

'I don't want to take advantage of your good nature any further, Rhian.'

In the end it was agreed that I would only be in touch if it was something important. He held out his hand and said it had been a pleasure to meet me and thanked me again for joining him. It was only when I was lying in bed later, listening to the wintry rain sting the window, it really sunk in that in six months' time I would no longer be Idris's neighbour anyway.

***

Spring was definitely underway. It was less than a couple of weeks until the clocks went forward, heralding an extra hour of welcome daylight in the evening. I'd been waiting a few days for a sufficiently good weather forecast to tempt me to start my trek of the Coast Path in day chunks, including a walk back to the car every time along quiet inland lanes and tracks. Today no rain was expected so it was an auspicious day to begin the project. I had broken the entire walk up into about twenty day-hikes, so if I did an average of one per week I would be finished by the end of the summer.

I was really looking forward to renewing my acquaintance with the local coast. There would be more time and space to savour each walk than there had been last year, when every day I had to be moving on to the next stage, with little chance to let the impressions I had formed take root in my being. This time it wasn't to be a linear journey, but it would still be a pilgrimage, of sorts, I liked to think. A pilgrimage: *the external manifestation of an internal journey*. I had read that somewhere a few years ago and it had resonated with me. When you leave most of your life behind for a while and concentrate solely on the physical endeavour of getting yourself between the start-point and the end-point for the day, with all the supplementary resting, re-fuelling and tending your kit, then normal life takes a back seat and the internal journey opens itself to you. What is this internal journey? Well, for me it involves a feeling of peace and rightness; I feel like I am my most authentic self. I had been on several such pilgrimages for a week or two at a time, and I have always returned home spiritually refreshed. I remembered trying haltingly to explain that to Cameron. Wow, Cameron; that's a name from the past. Thinking about him only evoked feelings of something moved on from, of a relationship that belonged to a certain past time and place.

The reason why I hadn't produced an order for these day walks was that I preferred to be guided by things like the weather, for example the wind speed and direction. Then I would tick them off one by one, and finally assemble the jigsaw pieces of my second pilgrimage along the beautiful Pembrokeshire coast.

I was kicking off my walks programme along part of the Milford Haven coast, with a detour to a little church at Monk Haven. This was all because of a conversation I had had recently with Barbara. I had told her about my planned re-visiting of the entire Coast Path because I knew she would be interested and have some salient input.

'Ooh, how exciting!' she had said. 'I'd love to come with you, but I don't have your stamina.' I had made a neutral reply because I didn't really want her, or anyone, tagging along. It feels right that genuine pilgrimages are executed alone.

'And I can recommend the perfect walk for you to start off your challenge! There's an amazing display of snowdrops and daffodils at a little churchyard I know, only a stone's throw from the Coast Path. You have only about a two or three week window to catch both flowers to perfection together. I went the other day, but I'm ashamed to say I took the car to the church. I did walk down to the coast and have a look at it, though. Benton went in the sea, like he usually does.'

I caressed Benton's soft ear while I replied and asked her to point out Monk Haven to me on the map. Benton and I had become firm friends over the months, and we both liked seeing one another. I am OK with other people's dogs, but I have no wish to own one myself. In my life now I am trying to be tied down as little as possible.

So, armed with Barbara's local knowledge, I took the road south and parked near a little inlet known as Sandy Haven, which is off the main Milford Haven. My boots were disturbingly pristine and probably the cleanest they would be for all the forthcoming season since I had recently given them a good freshen up and treated the leather with dubbin to keep it supple. I'm afraid I'm not of those careful walkers who has the dedication to keep their boots in immaculate condition. I actually like the way the mud and dirt accumulate; it's a memento of all the joyous walks you've been on. Or am I just trying to justify my laziness? Also boots become increasingly comfortable and bedded in as time goes by, the creases in the leather deepening like wrinkles on an ageing face.

I laced up the aforementioned trusty boots and strapped on my backpack which contained a packed lunch and other important things, picked up my walking pole and I was on my way. The acorn signs, used to denote a National Trail, led me on a wooded path out of Sandy Haven up to the Milford Haven estuary. This estuary is one of the deepest natural harbours in the world. Therefore I wasn't surprised to see some marine traffic, with a stately tanker being the biggest vessel on the water, its elongated profile dominating the scene. An oil refinery rose out of the landscape on the other side.

Although the refinery was not the most attractive feature on the Coast Path, it did have its own place in the environment of the estuary. The elegant slim towers reaching for the sky contrasted with the earth trail that was supporting my feet. The day was bright enough but still quite cold; acceptable for March. I glimpsed primroses here and there on the side of the path, proving that spring had in fact arrived.

I descended to the tiny beach of Monk Haven, distinguished by a castellated wall at its back. I didn't linger, however, because I was eager to detour inland to the little church of St Ishmael's. On the side of the footpath that led to it, the woodland floor was dense with snowdrops. It struck me that these were particularly late bloomers. I associate snowdrops with January or February, and images of brave little heads protruding through the snow. Perhaps their late appearance was connected with the type of soil or the microclimate here, I mused. Anyway, they were a wonderful sight.

It wasn't far to the church, which was secluded in the valley like a secret only the few were allowed to discover. I went up to the gate which led into the churchyard and stopped dead in utter astonishment. It was exactly as Barbara had described. The churchyard, with its higgledy-piggledy graves and small trees stretching up the valley, was richly decorated with an abundance of daffodils and snowdrops in equal measure. The result was an ecstatic synergy that neither flower would have achieved on its own. Every gravestone was surrounded and overspilled by this riotous medley. I stood quietly and breathed in the scene.

When my senses had taken in enough for the moment, I tried the heavy wooden door to the church and found it unlocked. I hesitated on the threshold, because I'm not much of a churchgoer. But this little place wanted to draw me inside. There were the standard pews, altar, font and other church features that are seen up and down the land. The feeling of serenity that enfolded me seemed to complement the splendour of the landscape outside that held the building in its hand. I had left the door open, so the natural and the man-made beauty juxtaposed. Or arguably, was the architecture inside a church really a consequence of human undertaking alone?

These were questions I didn't usually wrestle with, which perhaps was an omission for a poet.

Mam said I had to go to Sunday School every week or God would get cross. But it was boring. It was alright when it was your birthday, because then you could put flags in the sand. It was like being at Barry Island except that the sand was in a big square biscuit tin, not on the beach, and if you were four you had to stand up four flags and if you were five you stood up five. If you were more than five you had to go to the big church. The seats were hard and you had to sit still or God would be cross. He got cross a lot. But if your Sunday shoes were nice ones you could look at them so you weren't so bored all the time. Mine were red ones with bows on.

There was a Visitors' Book in the church and I spent some time reading the comments. It surprised and rather pleased me that several of the entries were from travellers who had made a long journey from other countries. The beauty and peace of this insignificant little corner of the earth seemed to have touched all the writers, at all times of the year. After some thought, I wrote *The exterior and interior wealth of this blessed spot combine to make it one of the most special places I have ever visited. I will be back next spring to witness the floral exuberance of the snowdrops and daffodils.* When I read it back it seemed a bit pretentious, but I could hardly cross it out. I hesitated long over the invitation in another column to put what town or country you were from. In the end I left it blank.

Chapter 14

'Hello, it's Rhian,' I shouted, as was my custom when I opened Idris's front door now. He had given me a key since he came home from hospital, which had seemed like a sensible expedient. Sharon came out from the kitchen, her yellow rubber-gloved hands held up like a couple of puppets.

'Hiya, Rhian.' She jerked her head towards the drawing room. 'He's in there.'

'How is he today?' I hung my coat up on the hallstand.

'Progressing well. The physio has just been round to put him through his paces.' She beckoned silently with her head, asking me to follow her into the kitchen. The room was tidy and smelling of bleach from the Sharon-style cleaning it had just received. She peeled off the gloves, which she laid over the side of the sink, and leant against the draining board. 'He's doing great apart from that he still doesn't like trying to go up and down stairs, which he should be doing by now. Of course, he's probably scared because falling down them was how the accident happened, bless him.'

'I'll have a go at encouraging him.' I said this reluctantly, because I didn't have much faith in my ability to chivvy him along. But I was determined that today was the day I was going to broach the subject of Tim. I felt we should be good enough friends that I could do this without impertinence; nevertheless I kept putting off having the conversation and the longer I rehearsed it in my head the more apprehensive I felt. I was pretty sure that Sharon didn't know anything about who Tim was.

'OK,' she said. 'I wouldn't make a big deal of it, though. I'll bring you guys some coffee, then I'm heading off.'

Idris was sitting in his favourite chair next to the fireplace, his stick alongside him. It was a proper walking aid now, not the quirky cane he used to sport. He was looking better every time I saw him, but he still seemed older than before the accident. It was partly because I now knew he was nearly eighty, and because he shuffled around gingerly rather than stepped out confidently like he used to. And his range of hallmark bow ties hadn't made a reappearance.

He gamely got to his feet with a smile when I came into the room and for the first time I didn't say 'don't get up'. He was supposed to move around. We exchanged kisses and settled down to chat. He was as upbeat and positive as ever when I asked him how he was doing; he was such a nice old chap. I noticed I had automatically referred to him as 'old'.

Sharon brought us the promised coffee and biscuits and told Idris she would be back the day after tomorrow. We heard the front door close behind her and Idris said, 'Now, Rhian, I've been meaning to ask you. How is your writing going nowadays?'

It would have been so tempting to be diverted by that question, especially since I was maintaining a quiet output of new poetry about which I would have been glad to have Idris's opinion. But I had promised myself that I wouldn't put The Conversation off any longer. So instead I said, 'My work is ticking along very well, thank you. But I don't want to get into that right now. There's something else I want to talk to you about.'

'Oh? That sounds intriguing. Is there some nice juicy gossip? You know I'm waiting for you to get yourself a boyfriend, Rhian.'

I didn't allow myself to be diverted by his teasing. 'I'd like to know about Tim.' When he didn't answer, I prompted 'Your son.'

He drew in a sharp breath and put his hands over his face. I ploughed on, feeling cruel. 'I met him here after you had been taken to hospital. I wasn't certain that you knew that. Then before he went home, we met up for dinner and he briefly told me a bit about his background and his life now.'

Idris slowly let his hands drop from his face. The ticking clock was suddenly very audible in the warm room.

'Oh. You hadn't mentioned it so I assumed you didn't know. Oh, my goodness.'

I put my hand on his. 'Oh Idris, don't be upset. I won't tell anyone here – not Sharon or anyone at The Harp.' I told him briefly of my time with Tim and summarised what he'd shared with me.

'He actually came out with it told you who he was and what he was doing in my house?'

'Well, yes. How else would I have known of your accident?'

'I thought Sharon might have told you. My memories of those few days are very hazy.'

'You see, I didn't know if you knew that I knew about Tim… gosh, this is getting complicated,' I said.

We sat in silence. I hadn't supposed that Idris would have been so upset and I started to wish that I hadn't said anything, or at least had introduced the whole thing more gently. Eventually he raised his eyes to look at me. 'Please don't judge me, Rhian. You don't know what it was like back in those days.'

It was my turn to be shocked. '*Judge you*? But of course, I don't judge you! It must have been horrible to…'

He gasped. 'Oh, bless you, my dear. I would have hated you to think ill of me.'

I grasped his hand again. 'Why on earth would I think ill of you? I just didn't want a secret like that always hanging in the air.'

'Do you know, I need a drink. Shall we open a bottle and then I'll tell you about my shameful past? But it sounds like you already know the core of it.'

He was starting to regain his aplomb, so I let the labelling of his past as 'shameful' pass. We could come back to it. We transferred to the dining room where Idris opened a bottle of red and I foraged in the larder to come up with some savoury snacks.

We drank and crunched on our nibbles for a few minutes. I was reluctant to start the conversation; I wanted to put the ball in his court.

'Are you ready? Then here goes.' He twisted the stem of his wine glass, staring into the dark liquid. I sat perfectly still and waited. When he did speak, it came out all in a rush. 'You see, I always knew when I was growing up that I wasn't like other boys. I was mixed up, to say the least, and I couldn't talk to anyone about it. Then when I was sixteen there was a teacher... well, I won't go into details but basically my father found out and all hell broke loose. He did his utmost to try to 'cure me', as he put it. I went along with it – I assumed I must have something wrong, like an illness. So I went out with a couple of girls, just to please my parents. One girl, Molly, was the daughter of my father's friend. She was nice enough. My father must have been pathetically grateful when Molly got pregnant, and a wedding was quickly arranged. I just sleepwalked through it all.

'The child was born. I was able to keep up my university studies due to my parents' money, and we lived with them. I hoped that the child would draw us together, but it didn't. Molly took to whining and complaining. She knew that things weren't right, but she didn't guess the reason. And you have to remember, I was only nineteen. A youth. Living the wrong life.'

I couldn't help but think of Lisa and Simon, and the effects of a baby on a couple too immature to cope. And that was without the effects of a father with a confused sexuality.

'To cut a long story short after a few months I couldn't face my failure any longer and I left. I had to live on the streets for a while, keeping myself the only way I could, or sometimes throwing myself on the mercy of friends for a few nights. The whole business of who I really was came out. You can just imagine, everyone was furious. And Molly was very hurt.' Idris passed his hand over his face and sighed. 'It was the low spot in my life. After a while my parents reluctantly agreed to carry on supporting me while I continued my studies. A divorce was hastily arranged and they provided some money for the child. Oh, practically and financially my parents stepped up, but emotionally? They never could accept the real me. Anyway, I graduated and got a job in a publishing house.

'I did visit Molly and the child, but not often, I must admit. Molly hated me, so you can imagine what it was like.' I nodded. I was transfixed by the sadness of the story that was unfolding. 'I

131

was really glad when she met someone else and married him. She deserved it. The new bloke put up with 'Uncle Idris' visiting a couple of times a year, especially since I brought money and presents.'

I felt I should own up that I knew this part of the story, and Tim's reaction when he found out who Idris was.

'I don't know if I was relieved or sorry not to be seeing the child any longer. He was a bright enough little chap. But he already had a father as far as he was concerned.'

'I think it's to your credit that you did see continue to see him, for the first few years, anyway.'

'I don't really know why I did. I suppose I felt my responsibility. I can't say that I actually loved him. Not in any straightforward way. But he was my flesh and blood, after all.'

Idris refreshed both our glasses. 'Well, time went by. I established my life in London and eventually met Bernard, as you know. You can imagine my surprise when some years later the boy just appeared out of the blue, no longer a child. So he flitted in and out of my life, but he was always a bit of an embarrassment, if I'm honest. I didn't know how to behave towards him, and of course I couldn't tell anyone. What was I going to say? "By the way everybody, this is my son?"'

'Did Bernard know about him?' I felt a bit nosy asking him, but we were friends, after all.

'He did. Dear Bernard, he was most sympathetic. But a bit shocked, I have to say. They never met.' He spread his hands. 'Well, that's my dark tale. So now you know.'

I saw with a qualm that he was looking very tired. His body drooped and his head was sunk on his shoulders. But there was something I wanted to ask, and I didn't know if there would ever be a better opportunity. 'I was just musing that you said Tim was your next of kin when you went into hospital, and you readily knew his contact details.'

'Ah, yes. Well, technically he is my next of kin, isn't he? I had named Bernard as my next of kin until he died. Then, just in case it ended up that I didn't come out of hospital, I thought I should give them his… Tim's… name. I had memorised his details for just such an occasion.'

There was more that I itched to know in this fascinating account, but Idris was definitely showing signs of being emotionally and physically depleted, so I said that maybe we had chatted enough for today. He didn't demur. I thought of telling him that I could see the family resemblance between him and his son, but I decided not to. I said I would see myself out.

***

I was taken unawares by the applause and cheering that broke out when Idris and I entered The Harp. I had telephoned to check they were cooking lunches that day and told them who it was for, so they were expecting him. It was the farthest he had walked yet, and I was amazed that he could do this – slowly, admittedly – after only a few weeks with a new hip. He had even resurrected a bow tie for the occasion, which was a sure sign that normality was being restored. At least, the new normal was with Idris being a bit slower and cautious, and using a properly functional walking stick rather than his previous frivolous cane.

We chatted with Brian behind the bar and stopped a couple of times for Idris to be told how good it was to see him, before we got to our table. It had a big 'Reserved' sign on it, scrawled on a piece of card. You didn't really need to reserve a table for a pub lunch in the week, but it was a nice touch. 'Well,' said Idris, dabbing at his eyes with a handkerchief, 'I didn't expect that. How kind people are.' I didn't contradict him, but I reflected on the nature and rules of pub friendships. Clearly Idris was popular and well-known, yet that hadn't extended to visiting him in his home when he was convalescing. The camaraderie finished at the carpark.

There was no cawl – my favourite – on the menu today so I ordered salmon and mash with vegetables and Idris settled for steak pie and chips. It wasn't the most imaginative of pub menus, but it was hearty and reliable. We chatted idly for a while, to give Idris time to reacclimatise, although he said that now he was back, it felt like he had never been away. It was good to see him gaining in strength and confidence.

Lunch came and was up to its usual standard. We treated ourselves to apple pie too, with a pool of custard. As we sat back with our coffee Idris said, 'I greatly enjoyed reading the latest batch of your poems that you gave me. You have real talent, you know.'

'Why, thank you,' I said. I tried to sound nonchalant, but inside I was delighted. It's true I was gaining in assurance as I wrote but, novice in the field that I was, I needed someone to validate my efforts, to let me know I was hitting the spot. Idris continued to fit the bill exactly. He was not sycophantic, and he would tell me if there was a line that was clunky or didn't sit right with him.

'I like the way you have interlaced your life, especially your present time here in Lewis Cross, into your work to give material that you can use in your poems. Tell me, does writing poetry help you to live your life? Like a sort of poetic diary?'

I considered. Did writing help me to catalogue my days? I'd never thought of it that way, but I suppose writing a poem did help me to reflect on my experiences. Or did my experiences shape my poems? The chicken and the egg.

'For instance,' Idris continued. I was impressed by the poems you wrote which resulted from when you were poorly in January. It struck me so convincingly, and brought back memories from years ago, of how the mind plays tricks on you when you are delirious. "Fever" is my favourite of those poems. I shall read it again when I go home.'

'I can read it for you now, if you like.'

'Oh! Do you have it with you?'

I got my phone out and tapped it. 'I have it on here,' I said.

'Ah, you young people and your phones. I think I've done well if I can send a message and the recipient actually gets it.'

And I was still young, as far as Idris was concerned, anyway. It just got better and better. I cleared my throat and glanced around, checking that the pub was nearly empty now before I started reading.

Fever

How remote it seems,
That time I had the fever,
A patchwork of dreams
Stitched by a phantom weaver
For a dream-believer.

Feverish, I saw
Things strange, unknown, mind-bending,
Obeying no law
Of thought but some unending
Sense of things pending.

Yet think: that junkie's
'Dream-believer' bit swam up
From an old Monkees
Song – one I'd rather dam up
Or find odd bits to ham up.

Truth is, there's riches
Beckon the dreamer, the drunk
Or mad, but which is
Real treasure and which plain junk –
That's the poet's click-or-clunk.

Idris closed his eyes while he listened, which I found gratifying. 'Ah, the Monkees,' he said. 'Pop music never was terribly much my thing, but I liked that bunch of young men. They sang jolly songs, and they were all so good-looking and sort of clean and wholesome.'

'So you liked my poem because it reminded you of some boys you fancied?' I was teasing. Mostly.

'Oh no, my dear. It's a fine poem which just happens to have brought back other reminiscences.'

Oh, it was a joy to have the old Idris back with a twinkle in his eye. I returned the conversation from personable boys to my poem. 'That type of poem is a *tanka*. That means five-line verses rhyming ABABB and with syllable count 5-7-5-7-7.'

'No, I did not know that. You are frightfully clever, you know, to adhere to such a strict scheme. Although, I'm not sure it adds to the reader's appreciation.'

'Yes, this is an unusually disciplined challenge. But I love the mental challenge. Also the rhyme scheme and the meter let you introduce all sorts of nuances, tonal subtleties, even ambiguities of meaning or attitude. And anyway, I've only got one reader.'

'That brings me nicely to what I wanted to say.' He took another sip of coffee, with irksome slowness. 'What's your tally of completed poems now?'

'It depends on what you mean by completed. There's several that I've sort of finished, but not entirely to my satisfaction, and I need to go back and rework them a bit. I've shown you most of the ones I consider wrapped up, and that would be about... let's see... thirty?'

He nodded. 'That's what I thought. Basically, you have enough work for a collection.'

'*What*? You mean... a collection, as in a book?' My heart was starting to beat faster. Of course I knew what a collection was, and that I was being disingenuous.

'Oh yes, my dear. I can see it on the shelves now, with a dramatic picture of our own beautiful landscape to adorn the cover. A compilation of poems inspired by your experiences in North

136

Pembrokeshire. What do you think?'

'Well, no doubt every person who writes poetry seriously dreams that one day… but I haven't had enough experience and… and… I wouldn't know where to start…'

Idris cut decisively across my gabbling. 'Now that is where I can help you. I still have pals in the publishing game and I'm sure they would be interested in a fresh new talent.'

'But Idris…'

'Don't think I'd be volunteering to promote your work if it wasn't any good. They would take my word for it that's it's worth taking notice of. It totally deserves publishing,' he finished firmly. It seemed that the oldened Idris I had adjusted to over the last few weeks had been swept away by this decisive character.

I didn't know what to say. It was so completely out of the blue.

'This is to say thank you for all the help you've given me recently. But,' he raised an admonishing hand, 'It's important that you believe your work merits being released to the world. I wouldn't be suggesting that you put it forward it otherwise. Standards must be maintained, you know.' His tone was stern, but his eyes were twinkling in a very Idris fashion. Me, all I could do was stammer my thanks while this ravishing prospect opened itself to me.

Chapter 15

'Is this your still your house?' Joe had asked after I opened the front door and let him run inside. Nathan followed more slowly. I assured Joe that it was definitely still my house. He stared around at the silent furniture. 'But you don't live here anymore,' he said, puzzled.

I waffled, uncertain how to account for the difference between a full-time house and a temporarily vacated house while not confusing him further. So it was apparent even to Joe that there was an aura of abandonment that was becoming embedded in the bones of my house. Nathan came to the rescue. 'She's living somewhere else for a bit and then she's going to come back here,' he said, nailing it in a simple sentence.

I went round all the rooms throwing open the windows to allow the agile late April air to diffuse in and displace its stale February counterpart. I had become used to feeling like a migrant when in my own home now. I hefted my suitcase of winter clothes upstairs. I had glanced at Nathan slouched in the corner of my sofa, but I didn't ask him to help me because he was engrossed in his screen and anyway the suitcase wasn't especially heavy. I emptied it out on the floor of my bedroom – woollies, scarves, gloves and a pair of boots. Joe jiggled half-heartedly up and down on the bed, more curious about me stowing my clothes away and starting to select others than anything else.

'What are you doing?' he said.

Because normally he was so taciturn, when Joe wanted to talk he was to be encouraged. 'These are winter things that I have brought back from the cottage where I'm living for a bit. I don't

138

need them now because it's spring, isn't it? And that means it's getting warmer. So now I'm going to get some clothes for spring and summer. Oh, I just don't know what to take. Will you help me?'

Joe jumped off the bed and came over to pull out various tee shirts and shorts, especially the brightly coloured ones. I found my two swimsuits and asked him which one he thought should go with me. Not surprisingly he passed over the plain black Speedo in favour of the polka dot fancy number. Was I going to the leisure centre, he wanted to know.

'Why, no. I'm going to go in the sea, when it gets a bit warmer. You see, there's lots of beaches near the cottage where I'm staying.' He wanted to know if the beaches had sand on them and I said many of them did.

He went back to the bed-jiggling. 'Can I come to your cottage and go in the sea?'

'Oh.' I paused in trying to slip the tatty old tee shirt that Joe had chosen back into the drawer. 'I don't know. We'll see.' As I came out with this time-honoured delaying phrase, it occurred to me that perhaps it wasn't such a bad idea. Would Lisa go for it? They'd have to get a caravan or something to rent. And Lisa had liked the little of the area that she saw at Christmas. On the other hand, it was my world, and did I really want it invaded? We'll see.

***

As it happened, I didn't end up broaching the subject to Lisa because she came up with something which chased it from my head for a while. We had been celebrating Simon's promotion. He had applied for the position of Head of the psychotherapy practice where he'd worked for some years past. It had been a nerve-wracking time for him the last few weeks because, although he was the only home-grown candidate, the post had to be advertised and you never knew who else might be in the running from outside. So it was a great relief all round when he actually got it, and I joined in the congratulations. Of course, I couldn't help but speculate if the

139

extra money that would be coming into the house would compensate for the extra stress and workload Simon would be under, and how that would impinge on their relationship, but he and Lisa both seemed over the moon with the news, so I put my mumsy misgivings aside.

We were sprawled in the living room, sated with good food and lazy amiability. Lisa suddenly said, 'How's Idris getting on? Didn't you say he had fallen and broken his hip?' In an aside to Simon, whom she was leaning up against on the sofa with her hand flopped on his leg, she said, 'Do you remember, I told you Idris is Mum's elderly neighbour. He's as gay as they come and outrageously camp, and nice with it. He plied me with sherry when I visited at Christmas, so he's made a good impression. Mum's taken him under her wing, haven't you?'

'He welcomed me into the area when I first arrived, and we struck up a friendship,' I explained to Simon. 'So the taking under the wing bit went both ways until he had his hip replacement and needed some help while he convalesced.' I was obscurely gratified that Idris had made a good impression on Lisa.

If I hadn't been feeling quite so laid back, and Lisa hadn't asked me how Idris was, I probably wouldn't have shared something that I really should have kept quiet about. As it was, I said, 'There's a whole other drama around this accident.' And so I told them everything, just as it had been revealed to me. I started with the bombshell encounter on Idris's doorstep with Tim, moved on to dinner with him when he told me about his early life and relationship – or rather non-relationship – with Idris, and the years after. Then I recounted the parallel conversation with Idris where I heard his side of the story, and how devastating it had all been for him.

They listened with gratifying amazement, and I must somewhat shamefacedly admit that I basked in being centre-stage to spill this sensational story. Not that I exaggerated at all; the facts carried sufficient charge without that.

'Well!' said Lisa. 'That's what you call a good bit of gossip. Don't you think, Simon?' Simon's response was more reserved, as you might expect from an experienced psychotherapist.

'It is an understandably tricky and painful situation for both of them, which from what you say seems to have been navigated better than it might have been,' he said. 'Have you discussed it with your neighbour since the first time he spoke of it?'

I shook my head. 'That's just it. It's as if the door has been slammed shut on the whole subject. I'd like to encourage him to talk more about it, but I don't know if I should. After all, Idris is an elderly man recovering from quite a big operation.'

Lisa nudged Simon, not very gently, I thought. 'Come on, Simon. You're the shrink around here, aren't you? What should Mum do?'

Quite wisely Simon wouldn't be drawn. 'Difficult to say without more information. Whatever happens, it's advisable to take things very slowly. He might not want to engage with the subject at all which, after all, is no-one else's business. And he's nearly eighty, you said?'

Lisa chimed in. 'Yes, I can hardly believe it. I would have put him several years younger than that. Do you know when his birthday is?'

I told her it was in August.

'Oh, when you're still in Pembrokeshire, then. You could do him a party. Oh, I know…' she sat up suddenly and clapped her hands. 'You could do him a surprise party and invite his son and family. That would be fantastic!' She leaned forward and continued to hammer her point home, even envisaging my persuasive conversation with Tim, the invitations, the catering, the other guests. And when I divulged that there would be a first great-grandchild by then, her enthusiasm went off the scale, even so far as to say that she would come down and help with the organisation. I wanted to bring up my recent conversation with Joe about visiting, but I could hardly get a word in edgeways.

Eventually Simon intervened, playing the psychotherapist card. 'In the circumstances, a surprise party would be a very risky strategy, even supposing that you could persuade Tim to come. It would be likely to be more of a shock than a surprise for Idris, especially given that his physical health is still rather fragile. I would suggest that a reconciliation between the two men ought to be well underway before a party is realistic. It could be detrimental for all concerned otherwise.'

Lisa pouted for a while and put up arguments, increasingly tenuous ones, in favour of the party. Simon won the day with his firm professionalism. I was relieved. Although on first hearing the surprise party idea seemed to have merit, once you looked below the surface, I didn't want to go near it. To head off the simmering sulk from Lisa, I said, 'Never mind. You can do me a surprise party when I'm eighty, if you like.' She frowned at me, still not quite mollified.

***

Reading, writing and walking: such an agreeable way to pass the days. May was my favourite month, what with new leaves, wildflowers cascading on the Coast Path and the days lengthening. Nature had shaken her skirts out and got down to the business of spring. From Ordnance Survey maps I had constructed a hand-drawn copy of the Pembrokeshire coast, and by taping the pages together I had made a reasonable representation of where the entire county was edged by the sea – in fact, where I was walking. I was rather proud of my map and had put it up on the wall. When I had walked a section, I coloured over the original blue depiction of the coast with red and put the date alongside. Then in my note book I wrote a log of each walk, included such details as weather, duration and any notable impressions or experiences. I can see that I was soon going to run out of adjectives to capture in words the magnificence of my walks. The plan was that my blue map would gradually get eaten up by red over the next weeks. Already there were three stretches of my chameleon coast which had changed from blue to red.

So far, my day walks had all taken me to South Pembrokeshire, simply because the weather forecast on those days, particularly for wind, had been more propitious in the slightly more balmy south. It struck me that the south part of the coast, while still being undeniably beautiful, had a different feel to the north with which I was more familiar because I'd chosen to make my temporary home there. Basically, the north was less populated and more Welsh. This wasn't just my perception; it was a fact. There existed a notional boundary called The Landsker, which divided traditionally Welsh-speaking Pembrokeshire to the north from 'The Little England Beyond Wales', the south where English predominates. This detail of history still seeps into the present because you find more English place names in the south. The Landsker is supposed to meet the sea in St Bride's Bay. Whereas we don't know exactly where it is, when I do that walk I'm going to choose my own spot and stand with one foot in the Welsh bit and one foot in the English bit.

In the back of my mind there whispered lines from a poem I had once read:

> I speak from deep in Dyfed, little Wales
> Beyond both Wales and England, where like snails
> Upon the sea's green leaf the shells and sails
>
> Of ships and saints once bustled in the bays,
> Busy as bees about their lawful ways,
> All raising up a honeycomb of praise

One of the beauties of my days was that not only did I write poetry, but I also read more of it now. This was not only so that I could learn from others' rhyme and syntax, but also just for the pure pleasure of the words, the way they could make pictures burst inside my head. And I might even be a published poet soon. I shied away from the thought, diverting my mental gaze elsewhere, so that I wouldn't jinx it. But my thoughts strayed back, sifting through my poems to settle on the best ones, and imagining what the glossy cover would look like on the shelf of a bookshop. Now that the dam in my head was breached, I might as well indulge my daydreaming to dwell on signing my name with a flourish on the flyleaf. But what wasn't an imagining was the email Idris had received back from his publisher friend after I had sent him a specimen poem. He said he would gladly have a look at my collection when it was ready. He did, he really did.

Meanwhile, the weather forecast for tomorrow was smiling on me so I was planning another day walk, another bit of the map to turn red. Which part shall I revisit? I was tantalised by choice and would spend a nice half an hour with my map later weighing up the options. And summer was not many weeks away! I would sit in the garden to have meals, walk the Path in tee shirt and shorts, sit on the beach and bathe in the sea. Starting my retreat at Heddfan on September 1st had worked out really well, because it meant the best was saved until last, a grand culmination. I felt breathless with all the blessings in my life right now and the bounty of summer delights beckoning on the horizon.

I made myself a ham sandwich for my lunch and sat down to check my emails as I ate it. I disciplined myself to look at them only once a day – alright, not more than two or three times – so there was usually a few piled up. A quick scrutiny of the subject lines showed that they included an appeal from a charity, special offers from a clothes manufacturer and a nice newsy letter from someone I used to work with. Not that I cared what went on back in the office; I had no stake in that world now. And there was also one from the company I was renting Heddfan from. My first thought was that they were a bit premature asking already for the rent for the final quarter, but I might as well pay it now anyway. But that wasn't what the message said at all. The email said they regretted that Heddfan would no longer be available for rent after 31st May because the owner was removing it from the rental market. They hoped I had had an enjoyable stay and that they could be of service to me in the future.

Chapter 16

I cried when Mam said we were going to move to another house. I liked this house. I liked my bedroom with the pink flowery wallpaper and my very own dressing table with a pink frilly skirt round it that Mam had made on the sewing machine. And I would have to go to a different school and leave all my friends. It didn't matter to the boys because they went to big school, so they wouldn't have to change. Mam said the new house was nice and that I would get used to my new school. But I didn't want to go, I didn't want to go.

The darkest hour is just before the dawn. Isn't that what they say? Tonight, the sky was completely veiled by cloud, eradicating any features. I have always found the presence of the stars and moon consoling, a reminder that that are bigger, more immutable things in the universe than your own problems. I clearly remembered having sat in my garden at night after John had left, and the pattern of my life had been swept away. The moon and stars had maintained their calm presence and kept vigil while I sat and wept. Gradually comfort had crept into me then, a reassurance that there were some things in heaven and earth that would never change. It was me who was to change. I managed to rebuild a part of my life and became stronger.

But there were no stars tonight. I had woken up around three o'clock, and after some time spent restlessly fretting about the news I'd had yesterday, I gave in and got up to take myself into the little garden, dressed in my pyjamas and coat. It was a tiny patch, the only features being a small lawn, a tall hedge comprising various rambling greenery, and a lone apple tree. I sat down in one of the two plastic garden chairs. The other outdoor furniture was a matching table with a wonky leg. They had been little used by me apart from the odd time last autumn when the sun had come out. I had planned to have many of my meals out here in the summer, and to munch my breakfast while I watched the fruit ripen on the tree. But that wouldn't be happening now. In less than three weeks I wouldn't be here. I couldn't get my head round it.

Oh, I had tried to get some more information out of the letting agents, to enquire about some sort of reprieve. It was even in my mind to offer more money. But all the woman on the other end of the phone could tell me was that the owners definitely wanted to stop renting it as soon as possible, and that they had 'plans'. Plans? What plans? A patio and jacuzzi at the back? An extension? A makeover? Surely they could have waited another three months. But Heddfan wasn't mine. They could do as they liked.

I had phoned Barbara straightaway to see if she knew anything, because after all it was she who had first told me about Heddfan.

'Oh no! To be turfed out with so little notice. How awful for you!'

'I was phoning to see if you had heard anything via your friend who knows the person who owns it.' I tried to subdue the alarm in my voice.

'No, I haven't. And she's not in touch anymore. Oh, poor you, Rhian. You could have come to stay with us, but our son's going to be here for the summer, you see, so there won't be a spare room.' A slight pause. 'You could come for a couple of weeks at the beginning of June, if that would help?'

'That really is very generous of you, but I'll work something out.'

'You know, you could always go back home, then find somewhere else to rent around here at your leisure and come back for another holiday. Would that work?'

I knew Barbara was trying to be helpful and I thanked her, but I wanted to yell my frustration down the phone. This wasn't a 'holiday'! It was... what? The writer's retreat that Simon had foretold? An alternative lifestyle? An escape into solitude? A temporary home? All of those? One thing was clear to me: this sojourn needed a full year to culminate in its decreed end point. This wasn't my choice. It was nature's. I needed to complete one full annual cycle: the changing length of the days, the trees bearing witness to the sliding of the seasons, the silent arrival of twelve full moons. This stable backdrop had nourished my writing, the poetry which was now timidly finding its way into the world.

I wasn't sure if it was just the effect of my eyes' accustomisation to the darkness or if the black blanket of the sky was gradually lifting, but the outline of the apple tree and the unruly hedge was becoming slightly more visible to me, and the bulk of the outhouse loomed at the end of the garden like a prehistoric animal. So: I had established (1) that staying put in Pembrokeshire to complete my undertaking, my contract with myself, was non-negotiable, and (2) I had to wrench myself from this place, Heddfan, and find somewhere else to stay. The uprooting quest for a new dwelling would start tomorrow.

From somewhere close by, maybe Idris's roof, came the piercing sweet cry of a single bird to begin the dawn chorus.

***

Dear Rhian, I'm so sorry to hear your stay is going to finish prematurely and abruptly. You must be so upset. Let me come round and comfort you. Shall we say around midday. I will bring liquid succour. X

It was not always that Idris replied to a text of mine, so I was touched to get his very typical response. It was in fact bang on midday when he knocked at the door and I let him in, noticing the minimal use that he made of his stick. He sank down in an armchair and put his canvas bag onto the specially cleared space on the coffee table. The sides of the bag flopped down to reveal the bottle of wine poking out. I had already put the glasses ready. No time wasted here.

'Right, tell me everything,' he said after we had got settled with charged glasses.

When Idris says that, you know you can tell him everything. He is eager to hear all the details, including how you feel. Even though he clearly revels in any news for its entertainment and sensational aspects, he is a good listener and sympathetic. He also likes to dispense advice, so all in all he would have made a good agony aunt, with his own page in a glossy magazine. Do they still have problem pages?

'Oh, my dear, how awful for you.' His whole demeanour drooped in distressed empathy. 'What shall you do?'

'Right now, I don't know. I'm still in shock. One thing's for sure, it's not going to be possible for me to stay here. So I suppose the only thing to do is to start looking for somewhere else.' I had already explained, to the accompaniment of vigorous relieved nodding from Idris, how I felt compelled to complete the year's cycle here in Pembrokeshire, so going home wasn't really an option. 'I started some research this morning, because I've got no time to waste. It was all a bit overwhelming, to be honest.'

'How so?'

I was glad to articulate my disorderly thoughts to him, to help process them. 'Well, first of all I thought I would look for a basic flat or small house to rent. Shouldn't be too difficult, I thought. All those I saw entailed a six-month minimum rental period. I don't know if any of that would be negotiable. I phoned up a couple of agents but they weren't too hopeful. Then I thought that another option would be a holiday let – a caravan, airbnb or something. Another Heddfan ideally, but I can't hope for that. Naturally enough, there were none with several consecutive weeks available to rent; the most was only a couple of weeks at a time. Then there's the cost, at summer rates. Even if I am prepared to hop from place to place, it would really mount up.' I shrugged feebly. 'So there we have it. I don't know what I'm going to do.' I didn't even try to keep the despondency out of my voice.

'Hmm. Let me put my thinking cap on,' said Idris. He was silent for a few minutes while he appeared to be contemplating his wineglass. 'Have you thought of advertising in an 'Accommodation Wanted' column or the equivalent on the internet? Or sharing a house? Or looking inland, say in Haverfordwest?'

I digested this. 'No, I haven't thought of any of those.' Was this a glimmer of light in my dark hopeless tunnel? If I hadn't been feeling so unnerved, I would have detected some ironic role reversal – him being the logical, capable one and me being distressed and disadvantaged. 'The trouble is, I'm pushed for time. In two and a half weeks I have to be out of here.'

'So let's see. Could you place an 'Accommodation Wanted' advertisement straightaway?'

I assured him that I could get on it today, both online and cards in local shops, etc.

'That's a good start. Now what else could you–'

'I've just had an idea,' I burst in. 'In a couple of weeks students will start to go home and there might be some possibilities there.' As soon as the idea exploded in my head other thoughts followed it. 'But it won't be 'til the end of June that students go home. And I don't relish the idea of living in one room in a house and sharing a kitchen and bathroom.' So virtually as soon as I conceived the idea, I was seeing the bad points.

'I've lived in such circumstances. It doesn't have to be awful.'

I blessed him for his optimism. I thought of the communal living in my own student days. Not something I felt I wanted to translate into my sixties. Still, beggars can't be choosers, so I didn't rule it out totally.

Then he had the best idea of all – ask Sharon. She was a fount of local information. So I determined that I would get in touch that very afternoon and ask if she knew of any places where I could stay, or whether she could make some enquiries on my behalf.

I exhaled a big sigh and felt the tense muscles in my body start to relax, no doubt helped by the wine. I got up and gave Idris a kiss on the cheek. 'Thank you so much,' I said. 'You've helped me to calm down, straighten my thoughts out and start to plan some courses of action. I don't feel so panicky now. We've made some planning progress.'

'Any time, my friend. Things have a habit of working out, you know. Not always as we would have planned, but they do work out. The world keeps on turning.'

Before he could get any more philosophical, I said I would make us both a sandwich.

'I'm sorry it's only cheese and tomato,' I said when I returned from the kitchen and put two laden plates on the coffee table and a packet of crisps.

'Simple fare is perfectly acceptable. All this thinking and drinking certainly needs something solid with it, so it's very welcome,' said Idris, his napkin, aka a couple of pieces of kitchen roll, tucked carefully into his collar to protect his spotted bowtie and his shirt front.

We ate in companionable quiet. I was mentally making a to-do list.

Idris put his plate down and wiped his hands, fastidious as ever. 'Now,' he said. 'After all that brainstorming, may I change the subject and engage you in some news?'

I indicated that would be welcome.

'I wasn't altogether sure that I was going to tell you, but it seems that some distraction might be good.'

'What is it?' I was puzzled, but not that curious, to be honest.

'Guess.'

'Oh, come on, I'm not in the mood for games. Hang on… it's not from your publisher friend, is it?'

He shook his head. 'The ball's in your court there. And I imagine that's where it's going to stay for the time being, until you get your immediate future sorted out. Then it's up to you to submit your collection for consideration. Now, do you give up? Shall I tell you?' He was agleam with gentle teasing.

In a neutral tone he told me that Tim had been in touch. Tim had phoned him, in fact.

I was a few seconds taking this in. Idris had not referred to Tim since when he had made the big reveal to me about his past, and I had not known how to approach the subject, so I had just left it and more or less put it to the back of my mind. 'Ah. What did he have to say?'

'He'd phoned up to see how I was, and if I was getting back to normal after the operation and its consequences.'

'That was nice of him.' I was cautious. 'And how is he?'

With careful, off-hand probing on my part I found out that Tim had wanted to know the medical side of Idris's recovery, which was reasonable given his profession. Then he had quizzed him regarding how he was managing his everyday life, and was he getting such help as he needed. It was quite a grilling, according to Idris, and it was hard to tell if he thought this was caring on Tim's part, or an intrusion. Apparently he asked if 'the woman from next door' was still calling round. I wondered how Idris felt about this phone call.

Ideas about the birthday party flickered into life again in my mind, but they would have to be put on the back burner while I got a roof over my head sorted. Along with my poetry collection. So I left it by saying that I was pleased Tim had been in touch. I think on balance Idris was secretly pleased, although he was playing it cool.

After coffee Idris put on his hat and coat to go, leaving me to the various aspects of my accommodation quest.

'You know,' said Idris while he fumbled to button up his overcoat, 'In the reviewing of your options that we did this morning, there's one obvious thing we didn't consider.'

I paused in opening the front door. 'What's that? I thought we covered all the possibilities.'

'I have a large house right next door. You could come and lodge with me.'

***

May was probably the best time to be walking the Coast Path, on account of the profuse wildflowers. Sea pink, sea campion and knapweed were some I knew the names of. In various places they studded the path verges, and the grandeur of the cliff walks was

151

crowned by them. But even though I was entranced by these delicate jewels, my favourites in their short season had to be the bluebells. They were at their zenith just a little before the other flowers that I mentioned. Of course, you could see bluebells in many other countryside locations. Yet there was something marvellous about seeing them in deep abundance adjacent to the sea, especially when the sun was out and the sky, sea and bluebells complemented each other to make up a dazzling azure world. Then there was their beguiling scent. I could often catch it on the wind before I saw them. Another competitor, in my view, for the best natural perfume was gorse bushes, which released their pungent scent when the sun encouraged them. Standing next to a bush and inhaling, with the sound of seabirds and waves in your ears, and the horizon a hazy tease, was almost sensory overload.

You might wonder how I was able to go and indulge in a coast walk like this when I was leaving Heddfan in less than two weeks. Well, I was rewarding myself today because I had managed to make some progress on unearthing my next temporary home. For the first two weeks of June, I had found and reserved a little cottage in Lower Fishguard. OK, it was quite expensive and only for two weeks, but I reasoned that it bought me some extra time. In fact, if push really came to shove, I could spend the whole of the summer hopping from one lodging to another according to availability. But I didn't fancy being as nomadic as that, and I certainly didn't fancy the likely cost.

I had viewed a couple of terraced houses in Haverfordwest which had a room to rent from the end of June, with shared kitchen and bathroom facilities. The middle-aged landlady of the first, bundled in a large stripey cardigan, had looked askance at a woman in her early sixties who was considering such a set-up. Just in case she'd thought I was leaving my husband, I felt I should tell her my story about Heddfan. She shook her head and tutted gloomily about 'these holiday rents and how you can't trust them'. She hadn't really got the point. At the other house I visited I was greeted by a friendly young woman with a chubby baby on her hip. She showed me the room, which was available from the end of June, where the present student happened to be at home. I only got a partial impression of a cluttered space where the window could do with opening, because I felt embarrassed to be gawping at a room where a young man sprawled on the bed, tablet in hand and clothes flung wherever. To be fair he didn't seem the least bit bothered about my visit. In both houses, the bathroom and kitchen were adequate, and it seemed like I would probably be the only tenant. It would do, at a pinch. Quite a big pinch. I said I would let them know.

I had also advertised online and in several outlets – no responses yet – and was still combing estate agents and holiday lets. I had done all I reasonably could for now, so this fresh spring day, full of sunshine and promise, was too tempting to ignore. Life was still destined to follow its course, even if not exactly how I had envisaged. Actually, I was surprised and rather pleased with how I was handling all this. After the initial shock I found that I was able to take an 'it is as it is' view of the situation and accept it, rather than fall into a paralysis of despair and panic. Idris had helped, with his pragmatic view of the situation. He must have faced some changes in his life.

I paused on the headland to take in the view of the rocky shore. I had chosen to walk from Solva, a coastal village with an especially sheltered harbour tucked in a ravine, round part of the St David's headland to Porthclais, an even smaller harbour which was off the beaten track, just as pretty as Solva but without any tourist influence in the form of eateries and gift shops. I descended past the sheltered waters into Porthclais harbour itself, where various small boats were bobbing docilely. It was a scene that recurred often around the Pembrokeshire coast, with only small differences. I sat down on a waterside bench and pulled out my pack of homemade tuna sandwiches and some fruit. The tide was in and the waves were making soothing, slurping noises on the shoreline. As soon as I started eating, a couple of seagulls landed nonchalantly on the wall near me. They appeared to be gazing out to sea but I knew they had more than half a yellow eye on me and, more particularly, my sandwiches. They were fun to watch and share the space with so I threw them a crust. They both rushed together but only one of them was able to gulp down the morsel. I took pity on the other one and made sure he got some crust too.

Idris had taken me totally by surprise when he had offered for me to stay in his house with him. He had tactfully left me to think about it, because I'm sure my reaction was written large on my face. In fact I didn't have to think about what to decide; I had instinctively ruled it out. Seeing Idris a couple of times a week made for a pleasant friendship. Me being in his house all the time was too much, way too much, time spent in close proximity to one another. I would have felt the same about Barbara, or indeed any other friend. I'm pretty much a loner nowadays, I realised. It was not an unwelcome thought.

I poured myself a cup of coffee from my flask as I continued idly to watch the gliding seagulls and the rough, tumbling hillside. There was a currant bun in my backpack too. The seagulls could forget it if they thought they were getting any of that.

I had pondered what to tell Idris so as not to hurt his feelings. After all, his offer was very kind. In the end I had decided on the simple truth, which is usually the best option. He understood completely. And I think he was quite relieved.

I loaded the remains of my lunch things into my backpack and set off to return to Solva, where my car awaited me. I had yet to examine all aspects of Idris's revelation that Tim had been in touch, and the accompanying resurrection of the party idea. All that was too much to think about alongside the uncertainty in my life at present, so I pushed it to the back of my mind. For now.

It was a good decision to have come out to connect with the coast today. My mind and emotions were soothed by the magic to be found in the places where the land and sea bumped together. When I had walked the entire Coast Path last year it had been July, too far into the year to experience this late spring freshness which spoke of summer just around the corner. I drew the sweet air deep into my lungs. Yes, I would do what I had to do to allow me to stay in this magical corner of Wales for the next three months. It was a no-brainer.

Chapter 17

As it turned out it was Sharon who came to the rescue. As per Idris's suggestion, I had thrown myself on her kindness and local knowledge. Let me see what I can do, she had promised. She phoned me the next day.

'Hi Rhian, I know a family who have moved out of their house but are not putting it on the market yet because it needs a bit of work. They want the exterior to be painted and a small downstairs shower and loo put in first. I know them because my daughter is – I should say *was* – in the same class as theirs. I know all about it because we used to chat while we waited to pick the kids up from school, and sometimes they would play at each other's houses. Nice family. Anyway, they wouldn't mind renting to you for a few weeks. All off the record, you understand, and they don't want much money. I've vouched for you and said how reliable you are. The house is in that new cul-de-sac off the main road. What do you think?' She was bubbling with eagerness.

What did I think? A few hours later I had liaised with the owners, got the key from the neighbours, and was gazing round the bare living room with Sharon.

There's something almost mystical about the hush of empty rooms. You take in the bones of the house, its structure, along with the scratches of living on the skirting boards and marks on the wall where furniture had lived.

'Lucky they've left the carpets and curtains,' said Sharon sounding like a stand-in estate agent. 'And look, you've still got the kitchen appliances, cooker and fridge, fitted in. Ah, no washing machine. That's a pity.' We had moved into the kitchen and were surveying the sleek white units and the gap of the ex-washing machine like an extracted tooth. I desultorily opened some cupboards and glanced inside. Not a crumb in sight. It had all been left very clean.

'I could pop to the nearest laundrette once a week,' I said. 'That wouldn't be a problem.'

'I could never manage like that with my lot. The machine's on every other day, what with sports gear and work clothes. You could also ask Idris if you could use his?'

'Maybe.' I shied away from the familiarity that suggested. 'Shall we go upstairs?'

The hallway was compact, as is usually the case in modern houses. Upstairs were three bedrooms, also as small as they could get away with, and a bathroom, a 'family bathroom', as it's referred to nowadays.

'Do you like it?' said Sharon as we headed back down to the integral living/dining room. I noticed that there was a window to the front and patio doors at the back, allowing plenty of light in. All in all, it was a standard small semi-detatched in a close of identical such properties. As such, what was not to like? It wasn't Heddfan, that's what. It wouldn't wrap around me and embrace me in the same intimate way. But could it be Heddfan number two? A new and different peaceful place? My summer residence?

Sharon was waiting for an answer so I said, 'Yes. Yes, I do like it. It just such a contrast to where I'm living now, and this is all happening so fast. I'm a bit bemused, to be honest.'

'Yeah, I get it. And what would you do about furniture?'

'I wouldn't have any.' I had answered promptly, without thinking.

'What? Where would you sleep, sit down, keep your clothes and everything?'

I took these one by one and ticked them off on my fingers. 'Well, I've got a z-bed at home – you know, a bed that folds up into a z-shape – which is perfectly comfortable. Then I could get a cheap plastic set of garden table and chairs. That would do. I would bring plates and saucepans and linen and things from home. And what else was there?'

'Where to put your clothes and toiletries.'

'Oh, that's easy. What a good excuse to have a 'floordrobe'. After all there's no-one to see a pile of clothes on the floor except me.' I could have told her that my last boyfriend was unimpressed by my small but pretty permanent floordrobe, and enjoyed seeing the gleam of interest in her eyes. Instead I said, 'I'm on my own; I can live exactly how I like.'

'Don't go telling my kids about this floordrobe business.' Sharon laughed, a bit uncertainly. She looked at me as if I were slightly mad, but for me all the ideas of how this could work were falling into place.

Just like that, the cloud which had been sitting on me lifted. I would cancel my two weeks in Fishguard, which had been due to start in less than a week. I would wing my way back home to pick up the essential stuff that I would need, the z-bed and what have you, and come straight here. The anguished weight of uncertainty was lifting from my shoulders to be replaced by this incredible feeling of lightness, as if champagne bubbles were bursting inside me. I spread my arms wide and danced around the open space.

'Sharon, I think it's all going to work out! I can't thank you enough.' I grabbed her hands and whirled her round the room with me in a crazy, loping, laughing reel. I was reprieved.

***

You know, there is an optimal size for a house to be, especially if you have only yourself to consider. The size of this one, which I had discovered was called Llanberis for no reason I could discern, definitely suited the summertime. In the colder months, when much of life was indoors, a snug, small as practicable dwelling like Heddfan was perfect. The walls drew around you and delivered an effortless cwtch. Now that it was late June and we had passed the summer solstice, Llanberis was showcasing its charms. The long hours of daylight saturated the rooms through the big windows, and the absence of furniture added to the sense of uncurling, of space

157

and openness and blooming. When you opened the patio doors, the distinction between outside and inside was minimal and the warm breeze wafted in.

Yes, I had settled in and I couldn't believe my good fortune. In fact, leaving Heddfan hadn't been quite the wrench I had imagined, because I had transferred my emotions to Llanberis, my new summer peaceful place. I had traipsed back home and loaded my car with the necessities for my indoor camping project, as I called it, plus a few goodies and fripperies. It was exciting! Lisa had been bemused at my buoyancy but, to my surprise, she didn't put up any objections to my forward plan. I guess she was getting inured to what she saw as her mum's eccentricities. Simon was too busy with his new head honcho post at his practice to take that much notice, but the boys thought it was super cool. They both wanted to know if they could come and do indoor camping too. I had replied with the standard, non-committal 'we'll see'.

I was up early, as I often was on these midsummer mornings. I sat with my first cup of coffee at my plastic table, in my plastic chair, and edited the poem that I had finished the first draft of last night.

Ferry

No reveries like mine for those on board!
I muse, think how I watched the ferry sail
On childhood holidays, asked 'Does abroad
Begin at Fishguard?' conjured up some tale
Of maritime romance, and ran to hail
Its prompt next-day return. Not so, I fear,
For most of them, the grown-ups, who'll avail
Themselves of the short voyage-time to clear
Some emails, grab some sleep, and have a beer

Or two. Else they'll have kids to mind, or work-
Related stuff to do, or problems now
Left back at home, they think, but apt to jerk
All sorts of memory-strings once they allow
Home thoughts to wriggle in. Makes me think how
Thrice-fortunate I am to have come through
Those things, and more, yet find that they endow
This latest, wondrous life-stage with a new
And just as wondrous promise to imbue

That past with future blessing. When I see
The ferry now, that tiny patch of white
Slowly becoming shipshape, it's for me
As if the idea 'life-as-voyage', trite
Though it may seem, does get the feeling right,
This sense of how a constant to-and-fro
Of lives, loves, homes, or crossings day and night
Would surely, at the right time, let me know
How much 'further beyond' my life might go.

There's all that to-and-fro-ness, the quick turn-
Around morning and eve, the sheer routine
Of traffic-loading, bow-doors and astern –
There's all that humdrum stuff, but then the clean,
White vessel heading out – *that's* what I mean,
How sharply they contrast, yet how one such
Mere turn-around can switch the might-have-been
Into the might-yet-be and do as much
To change a life as some magician's touch.

Would it make it to the collection? I wasn't sure. But it was becoming clear that I wanted to reflect every season of my year here, so maybe it would. Now that I was settled in Idris was urging me to write the introduction and get the whole thing together and submit it. I was nearly there. I was. What was holding me back? I guess it was the thought of that reply: *Dear Rhian, thank you for allowing us to see some of your poems. Although we did enjoy reading them, I'm sorry to say that we do not have space on our list...* I'm aware that the world wouldn't end if that happened, but it would be such a good outcome and finale for my year's writer retreat to get published. It would be a vindication.

On the other hand, there were plenty of other benefits from my year's sabbatical anyway. It was a chance to get work out of my bones, explore a quiet way of life, make a few new friends, get to know this magical part of the world. All those boxes were certainly getting ticked.

I jumped at the knock on the back door. I hadn't seen the workmen's van draw up at the house. It was only a slight disadvantage of living here that the men came most weekdays and worked for several hours, so I wasn't able to cavort naked round the house, even if I'd wanted to. They were as discreet as they could be, and it was only going to be a week or so longer, I estimated. The downstairs toilet and shower were already in place.

The construction team consisted of two men, a middle-aged wiry bloke and a lad in his twenties who hung around behind the senior guy. A fairly typical combination, in my experience.

'Morning, love. Cracking day.' He wasn't the talkative type. I agreed with him that it was indeed a lovely summer's day and offered to get the customary teas, both with two sugars. I knew that was really what they wanted when they came to announce their arrival. And that was fine.

***

Idris no longer felt it would be sensible to walk up the hill from Pwllgwaelod beach, so I had arranged to pick him up in my car and

161

we would drive to the beach. From there we had walked to Cwm Yr Eglwys and back, which was all flat. Then we had settled ourselves on the bench alongside the beach and I was carefully dispensing drinks from a Thermos flask, having remembered that the café wouldn't be open because it was Monday. I had even brought chocolate biscuits to grace the occasion. Idris was impressed by my forethought.

When we went to the beach Mam always had the Thermos flask. She even brought it when we went further beyond, not just when we went to Barry Island. The Thermos flask had a sort of green stripey pattern on the outside and it had hot tea inside. I had my own special little cup and Mam would tip the tea into it and tell me to be careful. But first of all Mam had to dry me with the towel because I'd been in the sea and I was all shivery. Then Mam would give me a Rich Tea biscuit, broken in half. It was broken in half so you could dip it into the hot tea before you ate it. That was called dunking. A whole biscuit was too big to dunk into my little cup. Sometimes you would dunk your biscuit for too long and it fell into the tea. Then Mam would get it out for me with a spoon. If she wasn't too cross.

Really, Idris was recovering from his hip replacement remarkably well, and I told him so.

'Mmm,' he said, sipping delicately from his plastic cup. If he found this a bit infra dig, he didn't say so. 'I can do most things now if I take it easy.'

'What about going downstairs in your house?' I was being deliberately provocative, because Sharon had told me he only went upstairs once a day, and still slept downstairs and used only the downstairs shower room. 'It seems such a waste of your lovely big house,' I prompted.

He sighed and said, 'I know. I can manage stairs in other places, but that's not where the accident happened.' I nodded sympathetically. 'But you're right. My house is big, much too big for me. So I think I might move to one of those sweet little flats in

162

a complex that they call 'sheltered accommodation'. There's a cord you can pull in every room if you should need help.'

A child came running up the beach from the sea. Her mum was ready with a towel, but not a hot drink, as far as I could see. Apart from them and a couple with a dog lolloping round on the sand, the beach was quiet today.

Idris took my silence for surprise, as well he might. 'In just a few weeks' time you'll have returned to your English residence. I'll miss you,' he said.

And there it was. My English residence. My home. This year was only an interlude, a bridge to my retirement. Yet my mind baulked at it.

'I will miss you too.' It was the first time we had both acknowledged this out loud. Across the bay the ferry, the big white boat, was moving sedately into Fishguard harbour. We both watched the slick manoeuvre in silence.

'I can see why you'd want to move. It does make sense,' I said eventually. Now is the time, I thought. There will never be a better moment than this. So do it.

'I understand you have a big birthday coming up in August. Your eightieth, no less.'

He picked up on my change of tone. 'Oh don't! Where have all the years gone?'

'Well, here's the thing. I would like to lay on a birthday party for you. We can invite all your friends from round here, and further afield if you like. I'll do all the arranging. We could have it in your house or hire somewhere. And it will round out my special year in Lewis Cross.'

His response didn't disappoint. He turned to me and clapped his hands, as excited as a child. 'Oh Rhian, how absolutely splendid! I love parties. A birthday party for me!'

'And I think we'll manage eight candles on the cake, but not eighty.' We were both laughing now, relieved to have sidestepped the emotional interchange. The way that my suggestion had gone down so well gave me courage.

'Idris, I think Tim might like to come to your party. And

163

possibly some of his family.' I heard his intake of breath. 'After all, he did get in touch recently to see how you were.' Still no reply. 'He might be interested that you're thinking of moving and have some useful input. Quite simply, he might want to come and celebrate your birthday with you.'

Idris looked down at his hands and flexed his fingers. 'Do you think he'd come?'

'I honestly don't know. But I'm sure he'd like to be asked.' The mum and child had packed up and moved off the beach, and so had the dog walkers. We had the bay to ourselves. The sea hissed inexorably forward as the tide rose.

'So I'll go ahead and contact him, shall I? And invite the others, if you make a list?'

Idris appeared to come to a decision. 'Tell you what, I'll agree to Tim being invited, on one condition.' I waited. 'Your poetry collection. You keep procrastinating about getting it finished and sending it off. You do that within a week, and I'll agree to Tim and his family being invited to my party. Do we have a deal?'

Chapter 18

I deserved today. I had been working damned hard for the last week, what with finalising my collection and emailing it off to the publisher, then starting to get my act together about these party invitations. Regarding the book, there had been agonised discussions with Idris about which poems to include, what I should write in the introduction and what the title should be. We eventually settled on *Phantom Weaver* for a working title, which was taken from the Fever poem. I have to say I relied very much on Idris's experience, and I am profoundly grateful for his guidance to a novice like me. The least I can do is throw him a memorable party.

As a reward for sending off the manuscript, today I was walking the bit of coast from Ceibwr heading southwards over some rough and occasionally steep terrain to Newport Sands. I was just starting the descent towards Newport, with a fine view of the local topography and good old Carningli rearing up behind to greet me. Further beyond Newport I could just see Fishguard and the big white ferry waiting patiently to begin its voyage to Ireland. I was on home ground. Today the sea was sparkling in the bright sunshine; a perfect summer day. I had my swimsuit and towel in my backpack so that I could take to the water at Newport Sands before walking back along quiet lanes to where I had parked my car. The blue coast on my map was being replaced with more red every week.

I finished the steady trudge down to the beach, which was dotted with a few people. I staked a claim to a patch of sand by throwing my backpack down on it. First things first: take off my boots and have a long glug of water from my bottle. I stretched my feet luxuriously and sensuously explored the gritty surface underneath them. I've always been a fan of sand on bare soles. I had told myself that I would swim straightaway so I rummaged in my pack for my swimsuit and struggled into it under my towel. Not that there were many people to see, or to care about, a glimpse of nakedness from me. I slapped water-resistant sunscreen on all the newly exposed skin that I could reach and I was ready. Before I headed for the shore, maybe as a delaying tactic, I checked my messages to see if Tim had responded. No, there was nothing except my original missive:

Dear Tim, it's Rhian, your Dad's neighbour. Well, ex-neighbour actually, but still only a short walk away. A long story which I won't go into here. Here's the thing. As you may know, next month is Idris's 80th birthday and I'm going to do a party for him on 18th August, at his house. He would really love it if you could be there, and hopefully your wife too. He said it would make the occasion for him. He's thinking very seriously about moving to a small flat in a sheltered accommodation complex, which makes some sense since the house is big and he's nervous about the stairs nowadays. You may have some useful input on that. He is very well, albeit a bit slower, and we still meet up regularly. I hope you and your family are OK. How is your new grandchild doing? I hope to be seeing you in August. Best wishes, Rhian.

I reread it for the umpteenth time. Not that it mattered now since it was already dispatched. And what I had put about Idris saying it would make the occasion for him didn't become any less of a lie with repeated scrutinising. It was a white lie, though.

The small waves stung my ankles with cold as I gingerly inserted my feet into the sea. I had promised myself that I would walk steadily and continuously into the water, temperature notwithstanding. However the reality of the situation changed the plan somewhat. I took several minutes to cautiously allow the sea to inch up my calves, then my thighs, then my hips, until I was

166

waist deep. I wasn't used to this. It still took a few more minutes until I went for it and submerged up to my neck. But after that the exhilaration, the emotion, of being a part of the gently undulating sea was more than worth all my trepidation. I could look back and see the people on the beach, munching their picnics and reading their books. I could see my backpack sitting alone waiting for me. I could see where the Coast Path that I had taken wended down to this sandy place. I even floated on my back and let my hair dip into the water, my ears gulping the rushing sound of the sea.

I was aglow with overspilling endorphins as I walked back up the beach, casting pitying glances at the lolling bodies that I passed. I sat down to dry naturally as I wolfed down my sandwiches, hungry from exercise, bathing, sun and party planning. Life was good.

It wasn't until I was walking back in the afternoon that it dawned on me there was no phone signal where I was, so I couldn't have got a reply from Tim, or anything else.

***

Jason, the younger of the two workmen, was up the ladder in his hard hat cleaning out the gutters when I pulled into the drive after my walk and swim. Geraint, the older, was reclined in the van with the door open, smoking a cigarette. We acknowledged each other with a nod and a short wave. I pantomimed a tea drinking question by lifting an invisible mug, and he assented with a thumbs up. Amazing how much tea this pair could drink, I thought as I got out the biscuits and waited for the kettle to boil. They were nice men though, and I would quite miss having the odd word with them after they had finished the job, which would be soon.

The sound of another van, identical to the one already there, pulling up outside caused me to pause in plating up the biscuits. An unknown man got out and sauntered over, hands in pockets, to Geraint. They were then both gesturing towards the house as they talked. The stranger had timed it right in terms of a drink, so when I went outside bearing Jason and Geraint's tea, I greeted the

167

newcomer and offered him a cup. He appeared to be a bit older than Geraint, but with the same strong physique and ruggedness typical of a builder.

'Yes please,' he said without hesitation. 'Just what I need. One sugar, please.' A deep voice and a strong Welsh accent.

'What do you think of it?' he said, smiling and pointing towards the house with his mug. 'Have you tried the shower yet?'

I told him that I used the bathroom upstairs. He took another giant swig of his tea and asked if he could see the new shower room, so I took him to it round the outside of the house, in case his boots were dirty. They didn't look dirty. In fact he was a notch up in smartness compared with the boys, as I called Jason and Geraint.

The small rear extension, that seemed to be present in all the houses in the close, now contained a compact shower room, complete with toilet and small wash-hand basin. He looked over it all, including opening and closing the shower door and running his fingers over the seals. Eventually he nodded his approval. 'Tidy,' he said, in typical Welsh fashion. 'Nice choice of tiles too.' They were a black and white geometrical design with here and there a fleck of red to break the uniformity of the monochrome. The floor was grey and serviceable.

I agreed with him on the tiles. 'Right,' he said. 'The outside work should be finished in a couple of days and then we'll be out of your hair.' He had taken his boots off in a slick manner which he'd obviously practised many times. I took the hint and led him through the house this time rather than outside, aware with slight embarrassment of the plastic furniture and my stuff spilling everywhere. He took his mug through to the kitchen and put it on the counter, thanking me for the tea.

'Would you like another cup?' I said. 'It looks like that one didn't touch the sides.'

He hesitated only for a moment. 'Go on, then. I'm finished for the day and another brew would certainly hit the spot.'

I invited him to the living room to sit down in a plastic chair. I drew more water into the kettle, slightly taken aback by my own impulsiveness. Especially since through the front window I could

168

see the boys packing their tools away in the van and getting ready to leave, so we would be alone. What had happened to the woman who thought that the typical local directness was threatening? Oh well, you can hardly withdraw the offer now, can you Rhian?

I bore in the refreshed pot with a selection of biscuits. He looked totally at ease sitting among my writing debris of laptop, notes, pens, books etc, with one foot resting on the opposite knee and his toes wriggling. 'You're short-term renting the place while this work is being done, right?' I assented. 'Are the owners putting it on the market when we've finished up here, then?'

'It was arranged that I could stay until the end of August, but I guess nothing could happen that quickly in terms of a sale, even if they started to advertise it next week.' I quelled my spurt of panic.

'That's true.' He looked around, seemingly unfazed by my untidy living arrangements. He gestured towards the kitchen. 'We refitted the kitchen here a couple of years back. And we've done some conservatories in this close. They're good, solid houses. Somebody could do much worse than buy one of these.'

'Have you been doing this job long?' Polite conversation over the tea seemed to be what was called for. He told me that it was his own company (as I had suspected) and that he'd started it twenty-five years ago. But now he was looking to retire and pass it on to his son.

'I can certainly recommend retirement,' I said.

'I might as well ask since I'm curious, but you can tell me to mind my own business if you like. What's a nice lady like you doing short-term renting a place with no furniture?'

So I told him a shortened version of my story, and I was then very gratified to bask in his practically open-mouthed admiration.

'Wow. That's amazing! You actually came to a place you don't know for a year, and you've finished up indoor camping here. I think that's awesome.' For some reason I had played down the poetry writing aspect.

I shrugged modestly and tried to hide how delighted I was with his comments. I took another biscuit and nibbled it.

'What do you think of living on your own, then? Does it work

169

for you?' He had stretched his legs out now and was looking even more ultra-relaxed.

I was surprised by the direct question and replied cautiously. 'Oh, I've had several years of practice now. On the one hand it has its advantages, on the other sometimes it can be... well, lonely. Although I haven't been lonely here at all this year. I've embraced the silence, you might say. And made some friends.'

'Embrace the silence... yeah, I know what you mean. And about the lonely bits sometimes when you live alone.' There was a ruminative pause before he finished the last of his tea and got to his feet.

'I'd better be going. I'm due at my son and his wife's house for a meal in an hour, and then him and me are going to the pub, like we do about once a week. I'll tell him all about you. And thanks for the tea.' By this time he was at the door and manoeuvring into his boots.

Just before he went, when I was seeing him out, he turned back and said, 'Oh, by the way, here's my card,' fumbling in his pocket to produce it. 'I know you said you're moving out at the end of August but have it just in case. You never know.'

***

The first thing I did after watching his van drive out of sight was to grab my phone and check for messages. There it was... he had replied:

Dear Rhian, how very nice of you to be arranging a birthday party for Idris. I believe my wife and I are free on 18th August so we should be able to come. Kind regards, Tim

I read it again, twice in fact, but there wasn't much to go on. It was formal, correct, but left a slight suspicion of wriggle room where he had said 'should be able to come', rather than something like 'we would love to come and look forward to it'. Well, he was probably busy when he wrote it, so I decided stop being so

170

suspicious and take it as a yes. I had fulfilled my part of the deal with Idris by submitting my poetry collection to the publisher he'd recommended, so he would at the very least accept gratefully that I'd persuaded Tim to come. Hopefully he'd be glad.

It was about time I washed the sea salt off my body. Since the new shower seemed to have been given the go-ahead, I decided to christen it. First of all I gave it a quick clean, then I fetched my shampoo, body wash and towel down from upstairs and ran the water. As I had expected, the flow was strong and efficient, not taking very long to get up to temperature. I stepped in and allowed the warm water to soak my scalp and stream down my body. I shampooed my hair, which since the last trim had completely grown out the last of the artificial colour and was now an unashamed, mature grey. It could be thought of as a symbol for the completion my first post-retirement year. The memory of work now seemed like another life, a vague dream. Was it really me? Another me, who belonged to that time, but has now departed.

I lathered my body all over. It was in good condition for its age, if I say so myself. And the new shower had certainly passed the test. I dried myself and went upstairs to the bedroom, where I took some time to slather moisturising cream on myself to counter the effects of the sea and sun. I stepped over mounds of clothes and dug through one pile to eventually select a dress and sandals, as a change from shorts or trousers, with a pretty necklace to set it off.

Back downstairs I sat down at the table to start thinking about the wording for the party invitations. They would go out by email soon, once Idris had concocted a guest list. But I couldn't concentrate like normal. My mind was restless, which was a far cry from my standard evenings for the last months where I would happily cook myself a meal and then settle down to a peaceful time alone. For the first time, I felt restless and in need of company. Was it a sign of a winding down of my retreat year and a move towards a more balanced life, more bright lights, perhaps? Maybe. This evening I didn't fancy pulling something out of the freezer to cook. I would phone Idris and see if I could persuade him to accompany me for a meal at the pub. If he wasn't up for it, I would go on my

171

own.

The business card that he had left stared at me from the mantlepiece. I went to it and picked it up, fingering its edges. If he had asked me, I would have said yes.

Chapter 19

It was the sound of little footsteps on the floor at the side of my z-bed that woke me. I opened my eyes and saw that Joe was standing there in his pyjamas, watching me with his usual serious gaze. I blinked and swallowed to moisten my sleep-dried mouth. What time was it? It was full daylight, so obviously it was morning.

'Is today the party day?' he said.

I stretched. 'Yes, it's today. We'll have to wear our best party clothes, won't we?'

'Will you get up so we can go to the party?'

I sat up and poked him playfully in his tummy. Joe didn't usually like physical contact, so you had to be careful. 'We don't have to go yet. First of all, we've got to have breakfast, then I think Mummy's going to take you out for a bit until the party starts. Perhaps you'll go to the beach again.'

He thought about this. 'Will you come to the beach?'

'No, I won't be coming this time because I have to help get the party ready.' It was rather puzzling that Idris's party had sparked Joe's interest so much. I had explained to him that it was for a man who was very old, not a children's party, but he and Nathan were special guests because Mummy had wanted to come. I hoped to myself that he wasn't going to be very bored and disappointed, because I knew that kid's parties nowadays included a hired entertainer or a trip to some fun commercial venue with pizza afterwards, rather than the jelly and blancmange I used to serve up for Lisa and her friends followed by a game of pass the parcel.

'Will there be a birthday cake at the party?'

'Of course. And you shall have a piece. There will be eight

173

candles on the cake.'

More thinking. 'I had eight candles on my birthday cake when I was eight. You said this man was very old. So why is he only going to have eight candles?'

You tended to forget that, even though Joe was autistic and found some things difficult, he was very intelligent and especially good with maths. So there was no fooling him about the candles. There followed a clarification from me about how much cake space eighty candles would take up, and how much lung capacity you might need to blow them out in one go, which I don't suppose Idris had. Then it transpired that Joe didn't know any person who was as old as eighty and didn't have much concept about what that was like. Perhaps that's why he was keen to go to the party; he was curious.

I hadn't actually invited Lisa to Idris's party. After all, she'd only met him once and it was a long way for her. It had therefore been a pleasant surprise when she had asked if she could come to the party and stay for the weekend. Simon wouldn't be able to join the family because he couldn't miss a Friday and a Monday from work. I expect the lure of the indoor camping option at mine had a lot to do with it as far as the boys were concerned. They had come complete with all their own camping mattresses and other accoutrements, and the whole thing was an adventure for all of us. Lisa had been very impressed with the house, and proclaimed that it was much better than the last one. I said that Heddfan had been ideal for one person, especially during the winter months. But I surprised myself by how half-hearted my defence was. I had taken to Llanberis. The thick carpeting, big windows, up-to-date facilities and lack of furniture were a contrast to Heddfan. And it was still in Lewis Cross. Pub, shop, beach were all still in walking distance.

Yesterday had been a grand day. I had taken them on a whistle stop tour to show off some of the local beauty of this place – Lower Town in Fishguard, Cwm Gwaun, Carningli and Newport included – and we had ended up at Newport Sands with our swimming paraphernalia. After we had enjoyed a dip with lots of splashing we ate a home-made picnic and in the evening sat on the floor of my

174

living room to indulge in local fish and chips for supper. I had shown off my map, and I think even Nathan was impressed. Only one portion of the coast was yet to turn red, and that was the part that finished at Cardigan, the start (or end, depending on which way you were walking) of the Coast Path. I had two weeks left to complete that final stage and do the very satisfying task of turning my whole coast map red.

We had all been sprawling on the beach eating our late lunch when Lisa had said, her mouth half-full of ham sandwich, 'It really is extraordinarily beautiful around here. And quiet. I get why you came here, Mum.'

I glowed. It was the old thing about wanting approval from your kids. And it was satisfying when they could share in what you saw in something. You felt justified. You felt that your choices were valid. Joe asked if they could have ice cream so I fumbled in my purse for money and sent him off to the café with Nathan to get cornets for all of us. Lisa and I sat companionably and enjoyed the wonderful ambience that Newport Beach was providing for us.

Lisa said, 'You seem very laid back about this party. Are there many people coming? Is there much left to do?'

I lay down on my towel and looked up at the pale blue sky, diluted with streaks of tentative cloud. 'It's all in hand. When I heard that you and the boys were coming, I decided to go for it and have caterers in so that I could enjoy the time with my family. They will bring everything and do everything and clear it away afterwards. Great, huh?'

'Great, yes, but isn't it a huge expense? Or is Idris paying?'

'The deal we struck is that I would pay the caterers for everything except the drink. Idris wanted to take care of that, so I let him. I see it as both a birthday present and a thank you present from me.' I then went on to explain that Idris had facilitated the submission of my poetry collection for publication, and he had been a ready ear for my work.

'That's fab,' she said. I felt it was something of a lukewarm reply about the poetry book, but then she had been in raptures about the local area and you can't have everything. Plus the boys

175

had just turned up with the ice creams so she was distracted.

'As for the guests,' I said, 'A surprising number of people have accepted, considering that it's the holiday season. There are his local friends, who you might expect would be there, and even some people from his years in London have decided to make the trip. And... guess who else is coming?'

'You don't mean his son said yes?'

'That's exactly what I mean. Tim and his wife both accepted the invitation. All thanks to your idea.'

Lisa tried to be modest but she was obviously pleased. 'And is it going to be a surprise for Idris?'

'No... I wasn't entirely sure how he would feel about it so it could have backfired.' Then I told her about how he used inviting Tim as an excuse to blackmail me into submitting my poetry collection, and we both laughed.

'Well,' said Lisa, 'I'm looking forward to meeting Tim. In fact I'm looking forward to the whole party.'

I turned my attention to the boys. 'See the big white ferry over there? It goes to Ireland. It's always held a fascination for me.' They looked obligingly. 'I used to come to Pembrokeshire on holiday when I was a kid. When I was about the same age as you, Joe. And you see, there was only a small train that went beyond Swansea to here. Sometimes we went beyond to visit my auntie in Carmarthen. Your Mum must have driven through Carmarthen on the way here. But the memory that's really special for me is when we went further beyond.'

Joe lifted his head from his ice cream. 'Further beyond what?' he said.

***

Even though it was quite an eye-watering expense, I was so glad that I had engaged caterers for the party. After Sharon and I, with some direction from the birthday boy, had set up chairs and tables in the house and garden all we had to do was look pretty in our finery and talk with the guests. Sharon's husband, an amiable giant

176

of a man, had put up happy birthday banners and other bunting. The two men who were servicing the event – in fact it was their own company – had brought tables for the cold buffet, which was at present coyly shrouded in covers waiting to be unveiled later. It was also part of their job to mingle constantly with everyone to see that their glasses were topped up. The caterers were dapper and neat in their smart, tailored uniforms. That they were obviously gay was something I hadn't known when I had engaged them, but it did seem to be a serendipitous touch.

Idris moved between the gathering people, looking flushed with excitement and every inch the radiant host. 'I hope he doesn't tire himself out,' I said to Sharon, who was dressed in a long gypsy style frock and looking fabulous.

'Oh, the adrenaline will see him through, and it doesn't really matter if he's exhausted afterwards. He can just take it easy while he recovers.'

I thought for a minute and decided she was right. She's a wise woman, Sharon, and I told her so. Just then Lisa came up to join us, also looking resplendent in a glitzy blouse and figure-hugging jeans. I had already introduced the two women to one another and they seemed to get on straight away. Sharon's boys were around Joe's age, and you could see them timidly eying each other up. Nathan was keeping himself to himself.

'Is the guest of honour here yet?' said Lisa, sipping her wine.

'No, not yet. But I'm sure he'll be here soon.' I said this with more confidence than I felt, and my eyes kept straying down the drive. A couple of people trickled in, but they were not anyone that I recognised. Probably some of the London contingent. I greeted them and waved them towards the house, which was part of my self-imposed job. The three younger boys had scampered off further into the garden. I was glad when Lisa asked Nathan to go as well to keep an eye on them, because it struck me that Sharon's boys had more confidence than Joe, and you know what boys can be like. I don't think Nathan was too impressed, but he went anyway.

The caterers, Ben and Jerry as I called them, approached our

177

group proffering bottles of wine and beaming jovially. That wasn't their real names, but they seemed to fit. I think one man's name might have been Jeremy. They both had short haircuts and perfect teeth. I accepted another glass of chilled white and swigged at it. Where on earth was he?

A roar of laughter escaped from inside. I decided that standing here watching the gate was ratcheting up my stress levels so I took myself into the house where Idris was holding court to a group of blokes. He looked in his element with glass in hand and face flushed. The pile of birthday cards plonked on the sideboard for opening later was mounting up. And then, I saw him in the doorway, hesitating on the threshold. I rushed over. 'Hello Tim,' I gabbled, overcome with relief. 'I'm so glad you could make it.' He looked as smart and urbane as I remembered. In his wake hovered a woman, plump and with a nice smile. 'Rhian, this is Mary, my wife,' said Tim. She murmured her hello and said how pleased she was to be here. I thought she seemed a bit ill at ease. Not surprising, really.

'We had hoped to be here earlier, but we decided to drive down this morning rather than yesterday. Not the best plan, as it turned out.' His eyes darted round as he talked and his smile seemed rather nervous.

'Never mind, you're here now. Idris...' But I didn't need to summon him, he was already there by my side. I watched them shake hands, hesitate, then lean into a quick, awkward man hug. Mary came forward carrying a small, wrapped present and was introduced. Oh, I so much wanted to eavesdrop on their conversation, having engineered this meeting, which was looking auspicious so far. But it wasn't my place. Instead I watched Ben and Jerry uncover plates of artfully arranged sandwiches, quiche and the like. A couple of eager guests were already approaching the stack of plates at the end of the table.

I wandered into the garden. The boys were playing with a football at the far end. Nathan had unbent sufficiently to be kicking the ball around with them. 'Food's ready, boys,' I said, and with whooping and cheering from the overexcited younger ones they ran

178

to the house.

I was similarly heading back indoors when a middle-aged man approached me and said, 'Excuse me, are you Rhian?' Another visitor from London, I surmised. He had the city look about him, even down to a red silky waistcoat under his jacket with matching handkerchief in the pocket. A bit warm for this sunny August day, I would have thought.

We exchanged hellos and he said, 'I'm Derek Drinkwater,' and held out his hand to shake mine. Derek Drinkwater. It was a vaguely familiar name, but it took me a few seconds to scan my memory banks, and another few seconds to do a double take at what I'd come up with.

'Oh,' I said, my hand limp in his vigorous grasp. 'You're the man... the man...'

'Yes, the man to whom you sent your volume of poetry. It's lovely to meet you, in your own habitat, as it were. Could we find somewhere quiet to sit down a minute?'

People had drifted in to start on the buffet so we were alone in the garden. 'I have to say I enjoyed reading *Phantom Weaver*. It's a nice collection.' His voice was rich, mellifluous and despite my inner turmoil I noted that he knew when to use 'whom'. He smiled at me benignly. You know you're teasing me, I thought. Just say it. *It's a nice collection but...*

'We would like to offer you a contract to publish it.' When I didn't say anything he added 'How does that sound?'

It sounded unbelievable, that's how it sounded. I was dumbfounded. Eventually I managed to stammer my thanks while I took some deeps breaths to calm my heart.

Derek sat back and laughed delightedly. 'It's not often that I get to deliver good news in person. I take it you're pleased. Old Idris and I go back donkeys' years. Back when I was new at this game, he was such a role model and a mentor to me. And a friend. So I took notice when you mentioned in your covering letter that he supported your work. And then when he invited me to his eightieth birthday party... I wanted to take a few days off anyway so it was the perfect opportunity for a trip to this lovely part of the world.

179

And to meet one of my future authors.' He looked at me astutely. 'Look, rather than take up any more time at this lovely party that I believe you've arranged, why don't we have a meeting tomorrow afternoon, to go through all the business stuff, sign the contract, and all that?'

Idris was still in conversation with Tim and Mary when I went in, all of them holding plates of food and looking much more relaxed than when they had first arrived. 'Sorry to interrupt,' I said, 'But Idris, could I borrow you for a minute, please?'

Idris and I detached ourselves from the group. 'You knew, didn't you?' I said.

Idris raised his eyebrows in mock surprise. 'Moi?' he said, 'Knew what?'

I threw my arms round him, plate notwithstanding. A sausage roll fell onto the floor. 'Oh, thank you, thank you. I can't believe it!'

Idris disentangled himself. 'Now wait a minute, Rhian. Please know that your work has been published entirely on its merits. All I did was promote and facilitate. I'm glad I can still do something, and I'm glad that you have had the opportunity to meet Derek in person. He's a good man.'

We didn't talk for long, because it was his birthday party, after all. But I did take the opportunity to ask him how it was going with Tim.

'Wonderfully. It's lovely to see him now that I'm perfectly fit and not languishing in a hospital bed. I was nervous about it, you know, in case he turned out to be all cold and standoffish. But then I told myself, he wouldn't have been likely to come in that case, would he? And it's a delight to meet Mary.'

'Your daughter-in-law,' I said.

'Gosh, yes. Just fancy that! And let me show you the magnificent present that they bought me. He led me over to the sideboard to see a small black and white photograph in a simple frame. Although the picture was grainy, as black and whites tend to be, you could quite clearly see the handsome young man holding the hand of the toddler. There was no mistaking who the man was.

They were in a garden with a house in the background. 'Tim says he found it in his mother's effects after she died. I can't say I remember her taking it.' Oh, and there's this picture too. He pulled out from his pocket a recent photograph of a woman holding a small baby and man standing by her side. 'Look – that's my grandson and that's my great-granddaughter. All these people! All this family I didn't know I had! Can you imagine? And Tim says they would like to come and meet me soon. Me – their long-lost grandad!'

'I'm so pleased for you, Idris.' I couldn't say any more; I was too overwhelmed. I had hoped the party and the meeting with Tim would go well, but I hadn't imagined anything like this.

'And it's all thanks to you, you dear girl. I am most terrifically grateful.' He gave me a hug. Then he said, 'I will see you now and again, won't I? You won't disappear from my life?'

I smiled. 'Don't you worry about that. You most certainly will see me again. Now if you will excuse me, there's someone I want to speak to.'

I told Tim how glad I was that he and Mary had been able to come, and what a thoughtful present he had given to Idris. He thanked me for helping Idris when he had broken his hip, and for throwing this party. We talked for a few more minutes, while I finally made my mind up whether to ask him or not. Then I gave the nod to Ben and Jerry to go round and replenish everyone's glasses. That done, I gathered all the guests into the same room and tapped lightly on my glass with a spoon to get everyone's attention. Then I stepped back and left it to Tim. Quite wisely, he kept it short, and finished his speech with a toast to Idris on his eightieth birthday. Sharon appeared bearing the birthday cake with its eight candles. After Idris blew them out, there was a lusty rendition of Happy Birthday. In English and then in Welsh.

***

I kept out of the way the next morning while camping beds were being rolled up and clothes gathered together. I could hear rather

181

irritated instructions being yelled from room to room upstairs by Lisa, and I figured I was better off keeping out of it. Besides which, I had an important phone call to make to the house owners.

After I had made the call and their stuff had been brought downstairs, we had a rather late breakfast. I basked in Lisa's congratulations about what a success the party had been. The boys had enjoyed it too; Joe had made some new friends and seen what an eighty-year-old person looks like. It was when the boys were upstairs looking for last minute items that had missed the packing that I told Lisa. She took it better than she might have done. In fact, I think she was half expecting it.

After I had waved them off I came back in and looked around the living room. I could see just where my three-piece suite would fit, and my coffee tables, and my bookcases.

Home: a curtal sonnet

Soul's dwelling, castle, place to hang your hat –
All these, and more, were roughly what I meant
By 'home' from time to time. Its sense would shift
With every life-stage, change of habitat,
Or moment of self-reckoning that went
To make me who I am. The latest gift:
This home-from-home turned home-at-last, this new
Perspective from beyond the cloud-filled rift
That lately fell across those years I spent
In other homes, yet now affords a view
More life-embracing as the last clouds lift.

Ingram Content Group UK Ltd.
Milton Keynes UK
UKHW021450180523
421969UK00015B/623